ELUDING THE BILLIONAIRE 1

Eluding
THE
BILLIONAIRE
CATE LANE

Important Note:

The following story contains mature themes, strong language and explicit scenes, and is intended for mature readers.

Cover Design by: The Book Cover Boutique
Formatting by: Lou Stock at L.J. Designs
Editing by: VB Edits
Proofreading by: Evermore Editing

ELUDING THE BILLIONAIRE

To everyone, who chooses to take a leap of faith, and live their lives in full color.

ONE

Katie

Present Day

The fast intercity train cuts through the lush green fields of the English countryside, speeding toward London. I'm on my way back from a weekend visit with my old school friend, Sarah. She's still one of my best friends and lives in Bath, one of my favorite places in England.

The weekend was fun. Sarah is always the life of the party and wouldn't allow anything less. Yet I still remain gloomy.

This weekend, I wasn't in the mood for flirting with random, hot, single guys, even if Bath does seem to have more than its fair share. It's probably one of the reasons Sarah enjoys living there so much.

My head dips sideways to rest against the cold glass of the train window while I continue to stare unseeingly at the blur of passing scenery. The slight vibration as the train zooms along the tracks is, in a strange way, soothing with the consistency of the unbroken rhythm. My eyes drift closed, and my mind wanders off along a well-trodden path of self-reflection.

I haven't felt much like dating for a while, and it wouldn't take me long to work out exactly when things changed. When everything shifted.

I do love living in the UK, in particular, London, with a historic building down every street, a pub around every corner, and the loyal team I've built in the new office. Carlson Publishing might be the family business, but my stepdad and stepbrother Hunter, who is the new CEO, don't give me a free ride.

It took a leap of faith for them to agree to let me head up the fledgling London office of our publishing company nearly one year ago now. My stepdad wanted to wait for me to get more experience before throwing me into the deep end. It's not that he doesn't trust in my abilities, but more that he's overly protective of me, like all the males in my family. I have three stepbrothers who take their protective roles seriously. Hunter is the oldest, Blake is in the middle, and Logan is only a few months older than me. Something he never lets me forget.

Hunter was the one who convinced my stepdad to give me a chance. He's my strongest advocate but also the most protective of my three brothers. It's just the way he's wired. He has always taken care of us like it's his life's mission. He's the one we ran to as kids when we were scared. The one we still go to when we have a problem.

I miss being able to wander into Hunter's office in Manhattan for a chat. His office door was always open to me.

More than that, I miss living in Midtown. It was so cool living across the hall from Logan, with Hunter's penthouse just an elevator ride away. Even Blake, who doesn't work for Carlson Publishing, had a place that was only one block's walk from us.

It's funny how, in my rush to leave the protective bubble of my loving family, I never considered how much I would miss them. The holiday season can't get here soon enough. In a couple of weeks, I'll be back in Manhattan for the Carlson Christmas Charity Gala, where I'll get to see them all again.

I release a heavy sigh, and a foggy circle momentarily appears on the train window. I wish it was just a case of being homesick that caused my somber mood. No, my unusually despondent outlook can mostly be blamed on a man. Not just any man, but a man I can't get out of my head. A man who sucked out some of the enjoyment of living in London, and what makes it worse is that I let him.

How many months has it been? I mentally count back to when I last saw Drew.

Damn. Five months now. Too long for me to have hope for any kind of future for us, but not long enough to forget him. Not that it's even an option for me to forget him because in the not too distant future, I will have to face him again for purely business purposes. I'm dreading it which is why I can't get him out of my head.

I can't believe that after all this time he's reached out to me only once via email. A business-related email at that, like we were mere professional acquaintances. There has been no personal contact, and certainly no mention of our last time together when we did a whole heap of very unbusinesslike things.

It's become increasingly clear with the passing of each week that, for him, it was all about the sex, and none of it meant anywhere near as much as it did to me. I don't doubt he enjoyed our time together. There was no denying our sexual chemistry, and he did track me down for a repeat. But then nothing since. Even now, my cheeks heat when I remember how easily I fell into him.

Over the intercom of the train comes an announcement that we will be arriving at Paddington Station in thirty minutes, and my eyes pop open. I pull my phone out of my jacket pocket and begin to scan through my work emails wanting to make sure that in the last couple of hours I haven't missed anything important. But I'm soon distracted by my earlier thoughts of Drew, and I can't resist rereading his email. Maybe it was churlish of me to reply with equal formality before advising him that I would be passing his request on to my chief editor. Let's see how he likes being brushed off.

I feel like such a fool for thinking, even for a short time, that we could have been more.

Sarah was right when she said I need to move on. She would know, being that she's always in and then out of relationships, none of them more than a few months long. With that kind of experience, she's mastered the art of moving on. I wish I had the same resilience my friend possesses. It's pathetic to still be stuck on a guy who I've only spent a few days with. Especially when he never promised me more than that.

The phone in my hand begins to vibrate with an incoming call and, as if I somehow conjured her up, I see that it's Sarah.

"Hey, girl. Are you missing me already?" I answer more cheerfully than I'm feeling.

"Of course. But I was really ringing to make sure you haven't forgotten your promise." I grimace, glad we aren't FaceTiming. I was hoping with all the cocktails she drank last night that she wouldn't remember the promise I made.

A silly promise that was part of a bigger plan to get my spark back. I think it was over our third or maybe fourth cosmopolitan that she said I needed to get back out into the dating world. And I vaguely remember that by the sixth, I was making a pinky promise that I would go on a date within the next week.

I can't hold back a heavy sigh before replying, "I haven't forgotten. But I refuse to get on one of those dating apps. Maybe I can ask that guy in the terrace house next door if he wants to go for a drink. Not that I even know his name. We've only said hello a couple of times."

"Good. I want to hear all about it. Remember, I know what you're like, getting all caught up in your head and constantly overthinking everything. Just do it. Enough of this wallowing in self-pity … I won't stand for it." This has me laughing out loud, and a few passengers in the nearby seats turn and stare.

I duck my head and whisper into my cell. "I need to go. We'll speak soon, and thanks for this weekend."

I disconnect the call and tap my cell to my head. Why did I promise to date someone? I *really* don't want to.

I've dated on and off in the past, and I've even had three relationships that could be classified as serious. The longest one went for more than two years until we realized that life away from the good times vibe at college wasn't really going to work for us. He had his career to work on and I had mine. At least I can proudly say that my breakups were all amicable. You just know when things aren't working anymore and it's time to call it quits. Luckily for me, they knew it wasn't working either. Staying friends after a breakup means no awkward meetings in the future. That was my golden rule until Drew, but he's made it impossible to do that.

Yes, Sarah is right. After five months, it's time I dated again. And trying to knock thoughts of Drew out of my head with my cell is only going to give me a bigger headache.

I drop my hand back to my lap and scroll to the selfies on my phone, all of which were snapped sometime last night. I can't hold back a smile as I look through the set of photos. Each photo is goofier than the last and a record of the number of cocktails we downed as the night went on. I flick back to the photo we took earlier in the day. Our heads pushed close together, my friend's blond, shoulder-length waves in stark contrast to my straight, dark longer strands, and her bright blue eyes the complete opposite to my darker brown ones. Opposites in looks and, I guess, personalities. Sarah has always been the loud, party-loving, good-time girl. I'm quieter. Reserved—almost shy—but always happy to let my friends lead me astray.

Sarah and I have been best friends since elementary school, our families living within a block of each other in Manhattan. Then, in high school, when Sarah's parents moved back to their home in England, she begged them to let her stay on as a boarder for her final year. They relented, and that was how we met Allie, my other best friend from school. The three of us were inseparable that final year and became known as the Glamazons. A stupid nickname really, but I guess if we had to have a label, it was a pretty cool one. It was also accurate, given that we loved fashion and were the three tallest girls in the senior class.

The jocks loved us while the cheerleaders hated us. And we became a target for some of their nastier comments. None of it really bothered us, though, as we had each other. The backing of Logan helped too. No one dared to say anything bad about me for fear of being ostracized by my brother and his friends.

Logan, like Hunter and Blake, was a sports legend in our school. Track and field, basketball, and swimming. You name a sport, and my brothers excelled at it. Especially as they all grew in their teens to be around six foot five. Funny how I never felt tall in my family.

Thoughts of our teen years together remind me that I need to call Allie later tonight. I wonder how things are going between her and Logan now that she's no longer his reluctant roommate and is instead living across the hall from him in my old apartment.

To say those two don't get along would be an understatement.

***

Later that night, lying in my bed in the dark, I release a heavy sigh. I've been sighing a lot lately, and tonight's sigh is filled with the frustration of not being able to get to sleep. My mind is still stuck like a broken record on thoughts of Drew. I really needed this weekend away from my flat in Kensington, but now, back at home, I feel lonely. I never felt like this before I met him. My flat was my sanctuary, and my life was full of new experiences and new friends. I don't remember even thinking about dating anyone in those first few months. I didn't have time. There was so much to fill my days with, like settling into a new country and a new senior executive role.

Before moving to London, I would probably have called myself a casual dater. Just like the next girl, I enjoy going out to dinner with a nice guy, but I can honestly say few have tempted me beyond a dinner date. My Mr. Right just hasn't come along yet. I've never even given all that much thought to settling down. But since Drew, my head is stuck on the idea of having my own special someone waiting for me when I come home at the end of a busy day. It could just be an age thing. After all, I'll be thirty next year.

My eyes drift closed, and memories of the first time I met Drew flicker to life, like one of those old movie reels I love watching while I'm curled up on my sofa.

But unlike those movies, it pains me to think that Drew and I don't have a happy ending.

TWO

Katie

Eight Months Before

"Let's party," Sarah shouts as she raises her cocktail glass high, then takes a sip. I smile broadly back at her, and following her lead, I take a sip of my own fizzy pink drink.

Before I can put my glass back down, she shouts again, "Come on!" Then reaches for my hand, and we race toward the dance floor. I'm struggling to hear her over the pounding beat of the music coming from tonight's DJ, but her intent can't be mistaken. It's time to dance.

The music blares out from the huge speakers at each end of

the temporary stage, reverberating and swirling around the mass of people already gyrating on the dance floor. Sarah flings her arms above her head, her blond hair glowing pink, then blue in the strobing lights. My best friend dances like nobody's watching, and I love her total disregard for social norms. Space magically clears around us, some people choosing to step out of the way, others—particularly the guys—just wanting to watch her.

Sarah's always been the trailblazer of our group, while Allie and I bask in her effervescent glow. I could never be outrageously carefree like Sarah. Nor could I be as sexually adventurous as her, not with my limited experience. But when it comes to over-the-top dancing, I can do that.

I throw my head back, laughing at her wild antics before happily mimicking her silly exaggerated dance moves. For once, I can enjoy the freedom of letting loose from all the stresses of another busy work week. There haven't been enough nights like this since I arrived in London nearly three months ago, and it's time I rectified the situation.

Tonight, we plan on having fun. Nothing too wild that would cause word to get back to my family in the States, but just enough for a short stroll down crazy street. So far, our plan is coming together beautifully. We've slipped into party-girl mode as simply as putting on an old favorite sweater hiding in the back of your closet. Though our outfits bear no resemblance to old sweaters. Instead, our dresses are short, body hugging, and plunging. Sarah's silver sequined sheath is as shiny and gobsmacking as a disco ball from the eighties, perfectly suiting her personality. While my more subdued black velvet fitted dress feels like a sprayed on second skin. The V-cut at the front provides an ample view of the deep valley between my breasts, and the backless scoop skims tantalizingly low over my butt. It's very revealing, but I have no fear of flashing the room thanks to some strategically positioned tape, a must-have fashion accessory for every party girl.

These publishing awards after-parties are infamous, which is why I wanted Sarah to come to London to join me. She's so much more out there than I could ever be and will guarantee I stay instead of sneaking off to my room upstairs for an early night since the formalities for the evening are complete.

The opulent ballroom at the Grosvenor House Hotel has been transformed into the ultimate party venue. My whole team is here celebrating, especially after taking the coveted International Publisher of the Year Award. Hunter will be very happy.

I look up at the ornate ceiling with gold chandeliers that send out shards of pinks and blues as the colored DJ lights hit them from all angles. Mesmerized by the spray of color and too many cocktails, I spin around too fast, wobbling on my black patent Manolo Blahnik heels before tumbling into a solid wall of suited muscle. Strong arms wrap around my body and two large hands land on my hips, steadying me. It's the only reason I don't end up on my butt, flashing the entire room my barely covered lady bits.

My hands are braced on the arms encasing me, and I look up to thank my rescuer, but the words I plan to say end up stuck in my throat. The man is gorgeous, with an impossibly perfect face that takes my breath away but also simultaneously sends warning signals blaring. Damn, Michelangelo would have even been jealous of those carved features.

The perfection doesn't end there. Each dark hair on his head is smoothed back from his forehead, parted on the left, and holding their position as if glued in place. The devil in me wants to run my hands through it, ruffling it up, but I wouldn't dare as his steely blue-gray eyes remain laser focused on mine. The three-day growth on his sharp, lean jawline is almost too even to be believed. This man is flawless. His full lips part as if he's about to say something, but then close again as we continue to stare at each other.

This is the type of guy I usually avoid. But not tonight. Instead, I smile up at the hot stranger because it's been too long since I've been held in the arms of a man that I'm this attracted to. It's not like I'm looking for some deep, meaningful moments. I don't have time for that anyway. But a bit of flirtatious fun? Sign me up. This guy with a playful smile now tugging at the corner of those kissable lips is exactly what I need.

He bends so his head is level with mine, and a waft of rich, spicy cologne teases my senses. Those appealing lips are now closer, brushing accidentally or perhaps intentionally against my ear. "All right, lass?" he says in a throaty, immediately recognizable Scottish accent that sends a vibration of pleasure zinging through my body. I'm getting serious *Outlander* vibes.

I may have only lived in England for three months, but it didn't take me long to discover that the mellow but sometimes harsh sound of a Scottish accent is my favorite. My stomach clenches at the thought of that voice whispering dirty things in my ear in the bedroom.

Whoa, slow up, girl. Since when have I met a guy and instantly wondered what he'd be like in bed? Maybe some of Sarah's personality is rubbing off on me.

I take one step back from the tempting Scotsman. I don't know anything about this stranger, and I've been burned in the past by smooth words. I need to hit pause for a minute on my libido that's screaming for me to get him naked.

"Great," I reply, continuing to smile up at him.

"Ahh, an American … So, Miss America, can I buy you a drink?" While my step back put some space between our bodies, I've just noticed that we're still touching. I let go of his arms, and he drops them to his sides.

"Sure, Mister Scotland," I shout over the music, and his smile broadens again.

I gesture to Sarah that I'm going to the bar. She waves me off, more interested in the cute fair-haired guy she is now dancing with.

I look back at my Scottish stranger, and he holds out his hand for me to go first. When I'm in front of him, I feel his warm, light touch on the center of my bare back. My whole body tingles with the simple brushing of his fingers on my skin. That's never happened before.

He leads me over to two spare stools at the far end of the long bar. It's marginally quieter than the dance floor, but he still needs to lean into me when he asks, "What would you like?" I want to answer, *Your body*! Instead, I ask for a glass of champagne. He half turns to place our order with the waiter. From this angle, I can check him out in the brighter light emanating from behind the bar. He is a fine specimen of a man, which only reinforces my initial impression. He's too perfect.

I look harder for a flaw. He may be a little older than I originally thought, as there is a sprinkling of gray hairs daring to peek through the darker ones. His profile is sharply defined, with his high cheekbones and straight nose jutting out at exactly the right angles. His lips and a couple of small lines at the corners of his eyes provide the only softness.

His head spins back to me, and a smile pulls up at the corners of his mouth. "I'm Drew," he says as he reaches out his hand. I place mine tentatively in his and say my name before dropping my eyes down to where our hands remain clasped. His grasp is warm and gentle with a hint of roughness to the skin, and I notice a thin white scar running from his thumb to halfway across his hand. This is a man used to physical labor. Not at all what I was expecting, and I wonder what other surprising revelations hide beneath his perfect façade.

We spend the next hour chatting, laughing, and flirting in our secluded corner. I run my fingers through my hair and press my lips together while I listen to him speak. His thickly accented voice is deep and melodic, playing out all sorts of naughty scenarios in my mind. I find myself staring at his lips as they form words, and I don't even care that I haven't understood everything he said. To me, it feels like foreplay, so hypnotic and hot. I want this man with a need I haven't felt in months, maybe even years.

Drew tilts his head slightly, looking at me quizzically. What did he just say? I smile back at him, and he quirks his dark brow.

Flustered and confused, I blurt out, "I need to go to the bathroom. I'll be back soon." I can't admit that I have no idea what he asked, because then he'd wonder where my thoughts have been.

I dash away toward the bathrooms, detouring via the dance floor to grab Sarah's hand. In the relative seclusion of the hotel hallway, I look in both directions, then whisper, "I need some advice." Her eyes dance with amusement. "Drew, the guy I was with on the dance floor earlier … well, I want to take him to my room and do rude things to him. But I've never had a one-night stand or even ever thought I could be a one-night-stand kind of girl. I don't know what to do. I mean, how do I even ask him?"

Sarah throws her head back, laughing. "Girl, I say go for it. It's been months since you were last with a man."

I mentally count back how many. "Ten months, to be exact."

"Wow, that long?" She seems genuinely shocked to the point that I'm blushing with embarrassment.

I slap her on the wrist when she continues to stare at me, open-mouthed. "Stop that!"

"Sorry, it's just that it's a really long time. Anyhow, it only proves my point. You need to get yourself a man, and if this guy is ticking your boxes, then go for it."

I wish I had a little of the confidence that Sarah has with men. A flutter of nerves takes off in my stomach.

"I guess. He's smoking hot, even if a little too perfect. And don't even get me started on his delicious Scottish accent, which is conjuring up all sorts of naughty thoughts. But I just—"

Sarah grabs me by both arms, forcing me to look her in the eye. "Stop right there. You're overthinking this. It's just one night with one hot Scot, not a lifetime commitment. You said earlier that you wanted to let loose tonight, so get out there, drag your man to your lair, and do all those juicy things you've been thinking."

I laugh at my friend as she releases my arms, spins me around, and gives me a gentle shove back toward the ballroom. "Go on. Do it, do it, do it," she chants softly behind me between giggles.

Looking over my shoulder, I smile and say, "Okay, I'm letting loose." I shake my hands out to prove my point and stride back down the hallway, in through the ballroom doors, and straight over to where Drew is still sitting.

I slide onto the stool beside him, and I blurt out, "Would you like to go somewhere a little quieter?" He raises one brow, and I like that I've surprised him. I also like that I didn't chicken out.

It's easier than I thought to just come straight out and ask for what I've wanted since I first laid eyes on him. Sarah is absolutely right. It's time I took my party somewhere private.

A little less forcefully, I explain, "I have a suite upstairs … and it's hard to hear above this music."

His lips tip up slightly at the corners before he replies, "Aye, let's do that."

I've never had a one-night stand before, and at twenty-nine years old, I'm thinking it's about time I did. I hop off the stool, stumbling a little and bumping into Drew. Another zap of electricity sizzles through my body as his hand flattens on the center of my back to steady me. One simple touch and any doubts about getting this guy horizontal fly completely out of my head.

I mumble my thanks and then jabber on about my high heels making me unsteady. I don't want him thinking I'm drunk, because

I'm not. My thoughts have never been clearer.

I want Drew's body naked … now.

THREE

Drew

I'm a lucky bastard.

I lead Katie from the noisy ballroom along the quieter carpeted hallway to the bank of elevators. I'm pretty damn happy she has a room here in the hotel, and I can't dial back the grin plastered across my face. I'd been thinking about taking our chat private, and then she surprised me with the suggestion that we go to her room.

I could have sworn she wasn't a one-night stand kind of girl. Those pretty blushes that have stained her cheeks when I've mentioned anything remotely sensual this evening had me placing her firmly in the good girl category. Not that I wasn't going to see if she was up for a little fun by asking her myself.

“My ears are still ringing from the music,” she murmurs almost to herself before reaching to press the elevator button. Her soft, husky voice perfectly matches her attractive dark looks. I’m not sure whether she naturally has that smoky tone, or if it’s a result of having to shout to be heard. Either way, it has the effect of making me want to draw her even closer. But she seems nervous, and I don’t want to push her boundaries too soon.

Side by side, we stand silently, statue still, staring at the closed elevator doors. The easy flow of conversation has completely dried up, and I wonder if she’s changed her mind about inviting me up.

Where the hell is the damn elevator? It’s taking an interminably long time, and it seems that the longer we stand here, the greater the chance that I’ll be in a minicab on my way back to my friend’s house within the next twenty minutes.

No longer able to tamp down my building desire, I begin to softly stroke my fingers against the warm skin of her bare lower back. It’s as smooth as silk. And then there’s that spot that dimples slightly above the top of her butt cheeks. Man, that could become a favorite place to linger.

This dress should come with a warning. It’s subtle in the parts it covers and sexy as hell with how it displays vast tracts of skin for me to touch. It was those killer curves that I noticed from across the dance floor as she swayed her hips to the beat of the music. Her full breasts were tantalizingly outlined by the plunging neckline and threatening to escape from the confines of the tight black fabric when she raised her arms in the air. From that first moment, I wanted to gather her to me and nestle her peachy, heart-shaped butt flush against my cock. I just didn’t expect it to happen so quickly when she stumbled into my arms and my hands automatically grasped her hips.

Katie leans into me, and the tip of her dark, glossy ponytail brushes gently across my arm. I want to wrap my hand around those long strands and direct her pouty, sinful lips to mine. The thoughts this gorgeous brunette has me pondering are making my cock thicken uncomfortably behind the zipper of my dress pants. Luckily, I still have my jacket on.

The elevator finally chimes its arrival, and we step inside. Katie's exotic fruity perfume punches my senses fully for the first time, conjuring up thoughts of warm tropical nights. I can't resist reaching one arm around her waist and, with the fingers of my other hand, tilting her chin up to me. I search her eyes silently for agreement, and when she melts into my body, I bend to kiss those sweet lips. They're full and pliable, and the demanding response to my kiss is worth every second of torment from the last hour.

I'd planned for the kiss to be teasingly light, but the moment our mouths connected, a fuse was lit. Every swipe of her tongue across mine asks for more. Every pinch as she bites down on my bottom lip is surprising and sexy as hell. I want to savor this moment. But Katie seems to have other ideas.

She presses even closer, her body molding to mine. There can be no doubt as to the effect she's having on me as my firm cock nudges against her taut stomach. She grips the lapels of my suit jacket like they're her lifeline. Like if she lets go, she'll fall. I wrap her tighter in my arms, experiencing a similar need to hold on.

Another chime announces our arrival on her floor, and we spring apart. Katie steps back, then turns away to face the door, smoothing her dress down over her hips. I want to follow that path with my own hands, but something in her rigid stance tells me my touch may not be welcomed. Fuck, I have no words for what just happened.

How does she do that? Change instantly from sexy hot mess to the cool, calm woman before me?

The doors open fully, and she marches out. I follow more slowly behind, my hands deep in my pockets, trying to adjust my uncomfortable erection.

Confused, I watch her stride widen the distance between us. She may not want to continue what we just started, but still, I can't help admiring the graceful movement of her long, toned legs showcased perfectly from the hem of her dress to the tips of those lethal looking heels. After what just went down in the elevator, my dirty mind can't help thinking about how good her legs would look wrapped around my waist … or my shoulders.

I'm probably moving way too far ahead of myself here, and I should give her some space to reassess the situation. A chance to change her mind. Because I want her, but I also want her to be sure.

I could also do with some space to get my body under control. *Come on, where is the calm demeanor I was legendary for back when I was in the SAS*?

Katie stops at her door, pulling a keycard from a sparkly purse I hadn't even noticed hanging from a chain on her shoulder. Still, she doesn't say anything about what just happened. The door opens, and before she steps over the threshold, I place my palm lightly on her forearm. Immediately, she freezes in place. My body encircles hers, but I keep a space between us so we're not physically touching. Although I want nothing more than to hold her close again.

"Katie, do you want me to leave … or come inside?" I ask. It's important that I don't make any assumptions about what she's agreeing too.

I don't have the capacity to read her body language anymore, so it's easier to ask straight out. Before she answers, I send up a silent prayer that she won't tell me to go. It would kill me to walk away, but if that's what she wants, then I'll revert to my original plan to return to my friend Aaron's place in Ealing.

Her head turns slightly in my direction, and when those dark, mysterious eyes scan up to meet mine, there is a fire burning in them that matches my passion. I release the breath I was holding, but still I'm shocked when she grabs tightly to my tie and pulls me through the door. To think I wasn't going to wear a tie tonight. If I hadn't, I would have missed that sexy, hot, empowering move.

The door bangs shut behind us. Then, with both hands flat on my chest, she pushes me back against it. I've never had a woman take control like this … and surprisingly, I like it a lot.

I can't stand simpering females fawning all over me. It's the biggest turnoff. But then I hadn't considered the opposite approach either. This woman has ticked some boxes I didn't even know I had. She's strong-willed, gorgeous, and totally unpredictable. I wonder what she has planned next for us.

I don't have to wait long to find out. With a cheeky smile, she tugs my tie free, throwing it carelessly over her shoulder. Then she gets straight to work on my shirt, deftly slipping the buttons through the buttonholes, one after another. Her movements are quick and without the hesitancy she showed downstairs in the hotel lobby. I stand there, letting her undress me.

When my shirt is pulled open, she runs her hands up and down my chest in sweeping arcs from shoulder to waistband. Her touch is cool against my heated skin, and the concentration with which her eyes are following the path of her hands has me grinning from ear to ear. I shrug off my jacket, which is beginning to feel way too constrictive, and she wastes no time tugging my shirt down my arms. Like my tie, it's flung over her shoulder.

I want to touch her body too, but letting a woman take control is such a new experience that I don't interrupt. Her hands make one more sweep, then snag on my belt buckle.

"May I?" she whispers, and I almost laugh out loud. I've never had a woman ask so sweetly to take my cock out.

"Aye, of course. Take what you want," I tell her. She does, unbuckling my belt, then unbuttoning and unzipping my pants before pulling them down to my ankles, leaving me standing in only my boxer shorts. She stares down at my cock straining behind the stretch-cotton fabric.

"Impressive," she murmurs, almost to herself. I choke out a laugh.

Katie has become a woman of few words but lots of action. Kicking off my shoes, then dress pants, I wait for her next move. A tiny crease forms between her perfectly arched eyebrows while she continues to stare at my barely covered cock. I wish I knew what was running through her beautiful head. That greedy look she's giving me is pumping even more blood to the region that is the focus of her gaze.

I'm painfully hard. Her eyes widen before tracking up my abs and coming to rest on my face. Another one of those cheeky dimpled smiles spreads her mouth wide. It promises more than just wanting to look.

Rising onto her toes, she hooks one hand behind my neck, drawing my face down to hers. Then she roughly seals her champagne-infused lips to mine in another demanding kiss. Again, the moment our lips touch, a fire ignites between us. The kiss is hard and full of need. She opens to me and our tongues fight for supremacy in a passionate duel, each of us giving and taking in equal measure.

I want to capture her in my arms, but I would hate to restrict her movements in any way. Instead, I let my mouth show her how much I'm enjoying our kiss.

Her free hand slips below the waistband of my boxers, then her fingers try to close around me. A low groan of pleasure escaping from deep within my chest is lost in our kiss. My dick flexes with a burning need for this woman before the lady in question pulls back from the kiss, her eyes growing wider.

"Do you like my cock in your hand?" I ask, and she nods quicker than a bobblehead character.

"But … You're very big. I'm not sure you're going to fit." Her head tilts to the side and she begins to chew on her bottom lip. It's so cute, I have to chuckle.

"Baby, trust me. You'll be so dripping, so ready for me that you'll be begging for every inch to fill you up." Her eyes darken with lust, confirming that she likes me talking dirty. Good, because I'm happy to share with her all the dirty thoughts and words running through my head.

She taps a finger to her lips. "We'll see. But first, I think I might need to get better acquainted with your member." Another laugh bursts from my lips. For someone so unafraid to take what she wants, it surprises me that she seems unable to say *cock*. The woman is a contradiction between words and actions. It's intriguing.

"Why are you laughing?" she demands, and I'm sure if her hand wasn't currently busy with my boner, she'd probably have it firmly on her hip.

"No one has ever called my cock a member." She blushes, and it's fucking adorable.

Hold up. Since when have I ever thought of a woman as adorable? Especially one who's only going to be a one-night stand. Maybe I had too much to drink, and the combination of alcohol with her pretty face has me turning soft. Inside. Not where it counts.

A couple of seconds pass where I think she may abandon the whole idea of sex. Then both her hands go to the band of my boxers. She begins to drag them down, and a whoosh of air is released from my lungs. The fabric is no longer restraining my erection, and it bounces against my stomach.

Her gasp is barely audible, and this time, that's all the reaction I get before she's dropping to her knees before me. I swallow hard. I'm so fucking horny right now I can barely see straight.

I know I need to slow this freight train of lust down. But first, I want those sinful glossy lips on me, just for a few moments of bliss. The same as any guy in this situation—when a beautiful woman wants to suck your cock, you let her.

She readjusts her position on her knees in front of me, then wraps her hand around the base of my shaft, her grip firmer this time. Her pink tongue darts out to wet her lips before she leans forward to lick the drops of precum from my tip. I wobble. Literally. She licks me again, running her tongue along the length of me, like I'm her favorite kind of ice cream. My hands clench at my sides. I want to fuck her mouth hard, but I let her set the pace.

I brace for one more mind-blowingly long swipe of her tongue, and my eyes roll back. Then she finally seals her lips around me. It's a new kind of torture—the way she hollows her cheeks, sucking on the crown, then easing her lips farther down my stiffened cock. Katie's mouth is full, and her head bobs up and down several times, working me over, hard and deep.

"Fuck, lass, you have a dirty mouth." My head bangs back against the solid door. I'm holding myself up with my palms laid flat against it. My eyes close and my whole world disappears into this one moment in time … her sweet, talented mouth on me, slowly taking more and more.

Hell, I need to take control back or this is going to be an embarrassingly short evening. I entwine my fingers in her hair and tug back gently until, with a pop, she releases me.

"Hey, sweetheart, we need to slow down before it's too late," I grind out through clenched teeth. "You're too fucking good at that." She looks up at me with the most innocent-looking smile. I'm in so much trouble here. Everything about Katie is perfect.

I help her to stand. She's taller than most women but in heels, she only reaches my chin. I reach one hand to her jaw and tilt her lips up to mine, dropping soft teasing kisses to her mouth, cheeks, and along her jawline to her ear.

"You deserve to be savored, not rushed," I whisper into the shell of her ear as I bring my hands up to rest on her shoulders.

Then, slowly, I begin to walk her backward until her legs hit the end of the king-size bed. My lips return to hers in another steamy kiss. Her taste is becoming slightly addictive, but there is so much more to discover, like the beautiful tits she's thrusting into my torso. Not waiting another moment, I ease the thick straps of black velvet down from each shoulder until the top half of the dress is gathered at her waist, trapping her arms by her sides. Katie's deep brown eyes flutter closed, and a delicate whimper slips from her slightly parted pink lips.

My eyes devour her lush, rounded breasts and pert dusky nipples, their bare beauty far surpassing my earlier imaginings. These beauties deserve to be worshipped and lavished with kisses. With both hands, I reach out to cup the glorious silky-soft mounds that fill my palms to overflowing. I bend and capture one taut pink nipple in a wet kiss before circling my tongue around its peak. She quivers in my arms, and the sound of her moans fills the air. I follow the same pattern on the other peak, but this time sucking on the surrounding flesh so hard she'll wear my mark tomorrow. I haven't given a girl a love bite in years, but something in me likes the idea of Katie having a reminder of our night together.

My lips explore every newly revealed inch of flawless skin as I drag the dress from her body. Kisses are peppered over her stomach and from hip to hip, no patch left untouched. Her skin against my mouth is softer than the velvet fabric being removed. Her fingers burrow into my hair, pulling me closer. I consider that an invitation for me to continue, so I do. Reaching the junction of her thighs, I help her step out of the dress now pooling at her feet, then flatten my hand to her stomach and ease her back onto the bed.

I need a moment to again drink in the loveliness before me. Her gorgeous body is clothed only in the skimpiest sheer black panties. The underwear doesn't hide much, but still, they need to go. Quickly, I slip them from her hips and down her legs so every inch of her is displayed before me. My mouth waters at the tempting sight.

Katie leans up on her elbows. "Well, are you just going to stare, or are you going to do more like you promised?"

I smile down at her. "Baby, I certainly plan on fucking you so hard you won't be able to walk tomorrow."

She grins. "Ooh, I like the sound of that." Laughter rumbles up from deep inside my chest cavity, spilling out. I don't think I've had this much fun with a woman in years, especially one I just met. I didn't come out tonight looking to get laid, but I'm sure glad I'm here now.

Under Katie's watchful eye, I grab a condom from my wallet and sheath myself.

"Spread your thighs for me, lass. I want to see how much you want me." Her grin broadens, and she immediately opens to me.

There is nothing shy about her movements now.

FOUR

Drew

A sliver of pale early morning light peeks through the heavy embroidered gold drapes. It's just enough light for me to see the stunning raven-haired beauty sleeping peacefully beside me. One long, tanned, naked leg visible from hip to toe with the crisp white cotton sheet wrapped loosely around it. The navy brocade bedspread kicked down so it's hanging more off the bed than on it. In this setting, she looks regal, a beautiful princess.

I certainly don't fit the role of prince in these opulent surroundings. I'm just an ordinary man who grew up poor in a coal mining town in Scotland. I may have done well for myself, but I don't belong here. I should have left before we fell asleep. I would normally. But when she looked up at me with those big brown eyes after her third orgasm, I just couldn't.

I take a moment to study her face, her smooth, flawless skin, her high cheekbones, and the thick, dark lashes fanned out over them. Katie captivated me from the first moment I saw her, that sexy hot body was hard to miss, and I wasn't the only guy watching her with her friend last night. I'm just the lucky bastard who was in the right place at the right time.

What we did in this room felt like our bodies had always known each other. Who am I trying to fool? I wanted to stay last night, and for once, I want to be right here when Katie wakes up.

I swallow, and my throat feels like it's filled with sand. Carefully, I ease her arm from across my ribcage before slipping out of bed. I need some water. I should have thought to do this last night, but when you have a stunning naked woman wrapped in your arms, there's not much room for a lot of thinking. It was all doing. And by the time we'd finished, I was exhausted.

My cock firms at the memory of how good it felt to sink deep inside her warm body.

Not bothering with clothes, I walk naked across the deep pile rug to a table with several small bottles of water on it. Twisting off the top of one, I gulp the contents down. I glance back at the sexy woman who could quench a different thirst. The shape of her lush breasts is just visible beneath the sheet, her arm resting on the bed where, moments ago, it was laying across me. I want to slip back underneath her, run my fingers through those long, dark silky strands of hair currently spilling across the pillow. Maybe even enjoy her body one more time before taking her to breakfast. I have nowhere important to be, and spending a few more hours with this captivating woman sounds like a good option.

I pick up another bottle and carry it over to the table on her side of the bed. As I'm clearing space, her ID from the awards event slips off the edge and falls to the carpet. I pick it up and flip it over to read the name. Katie Carlson – Carlson Publishing.

Fuck. She's a Carlson. I drop it back on the table like it's on fire.

This changes everything.

How did I not realize who she was? There were enough clues, but I was too busy thinking with my little head instead of my actual brain. Shit, this is a massive conflict of interest and could jeopardize the months of work my lawyer and agent have put into negotiating my next publishing contract.

I need to go. I search and find my boxers, pulling them on so quickly I nearly trip. Next, my dress pants, which are only half zipped before I'm slipping my arms into the sleeves of my shirt. I don't bother to even button it up. Everything is being done in record time. I've never run out on a woman before, but I guess there's always a first. Snagging my jacket off the floor and my shoes over by the door, I spare one last glance at Katie before slipping quietly out of her hotel room.

At the elevator, I force my feet into my shoes, stuffing my socks into my pocket. The bell dings, announcing its arrival, and I step into the cubicle, still doing up my buttons. The smoky-gray mirrored walls reflect the disheveled look of a man making a frantic escape. I hate myself for running away, but I couldn't stay. Not now that I know who she is or, more accurately, what she represents.

I check my phone. It's just before five and too early for the tube. Instead, I book a minicab to pick me up. Shit, I should have left last night. I should have politely thanked her for a lovely evening and said my goodbyes, like I would normally do.

Out of the elevator, I stride quickly through the deserted hotel reception area, not stopping until I'm a little up the street where I told the minicab driver I'd wait. I text Aaron to tell him I'll be at his place in half an hour. He probably won't appreciate the early morning message, but it's better than banging on his door at this hour.

I like staying at Aaron's place when I'm visiting London. He's got a pretty nice two-bedroom apartment in a converted Victorian house, and these occasional visits are the only chance we get to catch up these days. Aaron and I have been best friends for as long as I can remember, and even though we live very different lives now, we'll always remember where we came from.

Bilston, a small coal mining village not far from Edinburgh with a total population of less than two thousand, was a place of some good and some bad childhood memories. Most of the good ones revolved around Aaron and the fun we had roaming the local streets on our push-bikes. The bad times almost entirely occurred within the terrace house I shared with my parents and four siblings. The closure of the nearby coal mine in the late eighties hit the town hard, and my father was one of the victims. Not straight away, because it took years for the hard drinking to take its toll on his body. He spent years taking out his disappointments on one of his children, or more often than not, his wife. Every chance I got, I escaped to Aaron's house. His was a similar terrace to ours but across the street and down two, and it was my own personal sanctuary.

Car lights cut through the drizzly gray early morning mist, catching me in the beams, and I'm jolted from my memories. Thoughts of Aaron always take me back to our childhood and where the unbreakable bond of our friendship was first forged.

A trickle of icy rainwater sneaks under the collar of my jacket, running down my back, sending a shiver through me. I pull it tighter. Shortly after, the minicab pulls up beside me with a small spray of water and I hop into the back seat, buckling up the seat belt. I'm so tired with the early hour and the little amount of sleep I've had. Katie wrecked me, and even knowing who she is, I can't regret our night together. I just hope she feels the same when she realizes who I am.

It's a twenty-minute drive to Aaron's house, and I slump back in the seat, letting my head loll back against the headrest as we speed along the A40 out of the capital.

And that's the last thing I remember.

***

Beep. Beep. Beep.

My body feels heavy, my brain fuzzy and confused. What happened? The hum of a conversation seeps through my brain fog. I try to make out the low words being spoken, but no matter how hard I try, all I'm getting is the impression of a man's voice.

Beep. Beep. Beep.

Fuck, I wish somebody would shut that damn beeping off. The loud repetitive sound seems to be imbedding itself painfully into my skull like a jackhammer piercing through concrete. I go to lift my arm to brush something from my face, but the slight muscle movement radiates a wave of pain up the length of it, across the breadth of my chest, and down my legs. And for all that, my arm, as if restrained, remains on the bed. At least I can tell that much. I'm on a bed with a pillow under my head.

Words form in my head and stay there, never making it to my lips. I press my lips together, but even that is impossible with something lodged between them uncomfortably.

What the hell is wrong with me? The first clear thought I've had races through my head. But as quickly as it comes, it disappears again, like the ending of an old black-and-white movie flickering, then fading to black.

Beep. Beep. Beep.

Slowly, my brain eases into consciousness with a vague memory of this happening before; the steady, constant beeping the one thing my mind clings to as I slowly awaken.

Where am I? forms on my dry, sore lips and escapes from my body, not as words but as an incoherent grunt instead. I can feel somebody standing over me, touching my arm, adjusting the sheet that lies across my body. If I wasn't so tired, I would open my eyes to see who it is.

Cool, refreshing ice touches my lips, a trickle making its way into my mouth. I pray this small drop of moisture will unstick my tongue and soothe my raw, scratchy throat.

A gentle female voice near my ear whispers, "Andrew, can you hear me?" I can't reply. "You've had an accident, and you're in the hospital." It doesn't sound like my mother, and she's the only person I know who calls me Andrew.

The stranger's voice continues reassuringly. "You need to rest now." So I let sleep take over.

Beep. Beep. Beep.

This time when I wake, my head feels a little clearer. I let the sounds in the room wash over me. I remember someone telling me that I'm in the hospital. The constant beeping and whirring of machines make sense to me now and don't feel so alien. I try to focus on the low murmur of voices near my bed.

Now *that* is my mother's voice. The need to see her face has me finally blinking my eyes open a sliver. Bright lights blind me momentarily, but with a few more slow blinks, my eyes adjust. I tilt my head toward my mother's voice. It's only a slight movement, but it causes me to feel light-headed and queasy, though thankfully, it passes quickly.

There she is. I press my lips together before croaking out one word. *Mom*. The weak sound has the impact of a starter's gun going off, and she jumps up, rushing to my side.

"Andrew, I'm here, my darling boy." The sound of my mother's voice settles the panic pounding in my ears. My mouth curves in what I hope looks like a smile and not a grimace, but as everything about my body feels foreign at the moment, maybe my lips didn't move at all. I don't care though, as my mother leans down and kisses me on my forehead before squeezing my left hand. I return the pressure weakly, wishing I had the strength to do more when I see the tears coursing down her cheeks. My oldest brother and younger sister are flanking her. My eyes track to each of theirs since this movement seems to be the only one that doesn't hurt. The concern on their familiar faces stabs me in the heart.

"What … happened?" I force the words from my mouth, desperately wanting to understand how I got here and why my body feels like I've had the crap beaten out of me.

My sister, the doctor in the family, speaks first. "Drew, you were in a car accident three days ago. Both legs and an arm were broken. Your arm is a clean break and in a plaster cast. However, your legs were pretty smashed up, and you needed a couple of operations to reset them with metal pins and plates." My eyes never leave her face as she lays out my injuries one by one. When she finishes, I let what bits of the information I understood sink in.

My brother adds, "Basically you're going to be okay. And just as pretty as before, once the cuts and bruises heal." I force a smile to my lips. I appreciate his clearer words and attempt to lighten the situation. It's been an old joke between us since we were teenage boys arguing over who was the favorite with the local girls. Aaron always won. All the girls preferred him to the Campbell brothers.

Thinking of Aaron, I grind out another word. "Aaron?"

My sister leans forward, patting my hand. "He's just outside. I'll get him for you." I watch her disappear through the doorway and return shortly after, Aaron right behind her.

He stands awkwardly beside the bed. "Hey, old friend. You look like shit."

A weak smile barely moves my lips. "Feel like shit." Speaking really hurts. Actually, everything really hurts.

I just wish I could give them all more than a few grumbled words when I notice how weary they all look. They're trying to mask their concern, but I can see in their eyes that they've been worried about me.

I have more questions about my injuries, but already, my eyes are feeling heavy. I know from injuries I sustained during my tours of duty in Iraq and Afghanistan that I need to rest, let my body heal. It's familiar territory, although this feels worse than anything that happened to me when I was on active duty in the SAS.

FIVE

Drew

It's been eight long weeks of poking and prodding by medical professionals, constant noise, and the stench of antiseptic. Not to mention the buzzing of machines and the low drone of other patients groaning or mumbling twenty-four seven. Even at the rehabilitation center, the rooms held four beds, and all were occupied with other guys who were similarly broken and damaged.

Finally, I'm free from it all.

Aaron brings his Range Rover to a stop outside the small cottage perched on the clifftop overlooking the swirling white-capped sea far below. It's a gloomy day, even though it's the middle of spring. We both sit, staring out the windscreen. I let the wild natural beauty of the place sink in.

Aaron unclips his seat belt. “Damn, this cottage is isolated. Are you sure you’re going to be okay here by yourself?”

I turn to look at him. I can’t believe Aaron is asking that question. He can tell I’m pissed; we’ve known each other too long for him not to. I push open the door and let the salt crusted wind slap me in the face and cool the flash of annoyance.

“Isolation is exactly what I want. If I could be embedded behind enemy lines for weeks on end and survive, then I think I can look after myself in a tiny self-contained cottage in Cornwall.” No more words are needed. Aaron nods, understanding, because he enlisted with me at the stupidly young age of eighteen.

We both thought running away to join the military straight after finishing school would give us something better than our shit lives in Bilston. All it did was replace one set of crap circumstances with a whole different world of fucked-up. Initially, it was fun—the training for the Royal Marines, the teamwork, and having my best friend beside me for all of it. But when barbaric bastards start shooting at you, it soon loses the appeal. And when your friends are killed by those same bastards, then it’s hell on earth. Aaron got out sooner than me. After four years, he took his big brain off to university to fight for justice in a different way—as a lawyer. I don’t regret staying in, applying to the elite SAS forces, especially as it led me to a very successful writing career.

Aye, life was fine until the accident. I use both hands to lift one leg, then the other to face the car door opening before placing my crutches on the ground.

Aaron springs into action. “Here, let me help you.” He’s out of the car and moving swiftly around it before I can stop him. He reaches forward to help me down.

“Well, pal, it’s about time I stood on my own two feet … literally,” I joke before easing my feet to the ground and standing.

He stills, becoming an unmoving mass of muscle in front of me, his mouth a grim straight line. He obviously didn't think my comment was funny. "What? Too soon?" I continue, trying to lighten the atmosphere.

"Too fuckin' right, it's too soon. You nearly died, and you want to make jokes." He shakes his head, and a flash of guilt hits me like a punch to the gut as I'm reminded of the minicab driver who did lose his life that night. A knot of anger builds when I think about the drunk driver who hit us head-on, instantly making the driver's wife a widow and leaving his two small children fatherless.

My head drops down, and I lean heavily on the crutches. "Hey, did you set up that trust account like I asked you to?"

"Aye, all done, and I've decided to chip in too."

My throat tightens. "Thanks." He steps out of my path and walks around to the trunk to get my bags out.

Aaron and I have always been about the same size. We're not heavyweight big, but still tall and strong. Since the accident, I've become a lot leaner with the loss of muscle mass. I can't wait to get back to working out properly rather than doing just the exercises the physiotherapist has given me for my legs and arm.

I hobble on my crutches, slowly and carefully, over the uneven, slightly sloping ground to the wooden deck that runs along this side of the cottage. It leads to the front door, where Aaron is now waiting with my bags, one in each hand. He knows better than to offer to help me.

At the door, I pull the key from my pocket and awkwardly push the weathered piece of wood open, stepping directly into the living area.

It took me a long time to find this place—the perfect cottage rental for me to continue my rehabilitation. Not that I had much else to do while stuck in a bed for the majority of my days. I chose it specifically for its remoteness, and so far, everything that I can see is exactly what I'd hoped for. I hate crowds, a hangover from my days in the military when groups of people in war-torn countries had me and my team looking for danger in every movement of a hand, turn of a head, or murmured conversation.

I look around the room. It's just like the online photos: Simple but comfortably furnished. No stairs, only that one up to the deck from the driveway. No near neighbors, the closest about half a mile back up the gravel road. Perfect, because privacy was my number one criterion.

I duck my head slightly under a low wooden beam, one of two running across the ceiling from one wall to the other. It's a typical feature of these older cottages, even if a little annoying for guys as tall as my friend and me. Nothing I can't live with though, which is lucky because I'll be here for the next six months.

Aaron steps past me. "I'll drop the bags in the bedroom. I'm guessing it won't be hard to find. This place is small." I laugh at him as he walks through the galley kitchen, then opens the door on the other side.

I turn in the other direction and, leaning heavily on my crutches, make my way through the living area toward the pair of clear glass doors at the end of the room. The view through the glass appears to be all ocean. An illusion created by the way the narrow wooden deck across the back drops down onto a sloping lawn, which ends about one hundred meters away at the cliff edge.

I lean against the wall to push both the doors open. A blast of fresh salty air assails my senses. It's so good to be able to breathe in and not have the sting of antiseptic or bleach invade my nostrils. I've had enough of hospitals and rehabilitation centers to last me a lifetime. I'm grateful to the orthopedic surgeons who rebuilt my crushed legs with rods and plates, but the recovery has been brutal. I'm so glad to be free of it all. Well, at least the daily medical interventions and that cumbersome frame that was screwed onto my leg. Now I only need to keep up with the exercises the physiotherapist gave me.

I breathe in a big lungful of the sea breeze, and it reminds me of the one summer beach holiday I had as a kid. It was with Aaron's family at Nairn, on the Northeast coast of Scotland. We were about thirteen, and it was everything I'd imagined a summer holiday to be. We didn't care that the water was freezing as we raced each other to it, our feet sinking into the soft white sand, leaving imprints that would be washed away overnight with the incoming tide.

Aaron joins me in the doorway, and for a moment, like me, he stares silently out at the whitecaps cresting the deep blue water far below. I wonder if he's remembering that same holiday. It was a long time ago.

"I found the bedroom," he jokes, "and you'll be pleased to know the bed is large. But then that means there isn't much space for anything else in the room."

"I don't need anything bigger," I mumble almost to myself.

"Remind me again why you didn't want to return to your larger private home in Scotland?"

"You know my family, and probably yours too, would never have left me alone."

He nods, then spins around, saying, "I'll bring the food in from the car."

I follow him back into the living room and take a closer look around my new temporary home. The living room might be small, but it has a sofa, a small flat-screen TV, and a wood-burning fireplace in one corner. On the opposite side of the room is a full-size desk with an office chair, which is where I plan to spend most of my time writing. I have a lot of catching up to do after my unplanned hospital stay. Now that I'm managing my pain better and finally able to move around on my own, I need to get back to work and finish my book.

With a grunt, Aaron shoulders the front door open and carries the large box of food directly into the galley kitchen. It's just the basics but should keep me going for about a week until I can get more ordered online. I'm going to be here for months, so the sooner I get things like food deliveries sorted, the better.

"Just put it on the countertop. I can put it away later."

With a shrug of his shoulders, he silently turns to do another trip to the car to bring in the remaining supplies. Near the doorway is a small table pushed up against the wall, and I ease my body down into one of the wooden chairs. With Aaron filling the space inside as he moves about, it makes sense for me and my crutches to stay clear. I wish I didn't have to sit by uselessly and watch him bring in my gear, but even I have to face the reality that it's going to be a long time before I'm back to full strength.

A few trips later, there is a pile of exercise equipment and a box with my office supplies sitting on the floor in the middle of the living area.

"Where do you want this stuff?" he asks, placing the last box on the floor.

"Just leave it there. I'll work it out later. Grab yourself a beer, and we can go sit out on the back deck." Already, I'm finding I want to be out on the small wooden deck overlooking the ocean.

Aaron wanders into the kitchen. "Do you want anything?"

"Just a bottle of water for me." Alcohol and the pain meds I still need to take for the next week would not mix well.

When we're both settled into a pair of canvas-backed deck chairs with cold drinks in our hands, I lean forward, tapping my bottle to his.

"Thanks for everything you've done to spring me from the poking and prodding of the doctors and nurses."

If it wasn't for Aaron, I would have been stuck in the rehabilitation center for at least another couple of weeks. And I couldn't have handled that for one more day.

He shrugs before clearing his throat and saying, "Just remember to arrange for the local physio visits. You've been making great progress. It's a miracle you can even walk."

I'm tempted to call him out on his mothering, but I know it all comes from a good place. And I really am grateful to my friend.

"What's a miracle is that I can walk at all with all this metal inside me," I joke. "I'm going to light up like a Christmas tree next time I go through a body scanner at the airport."

We stay in this spot for the next hour, comfortable to just sit together, only occasionally talking. That's how it is when you've been best friends forever. There isn't a need to say much.

But then, as the late afternoon sun drops lower in the sky, Aaron stands with a sigh. "I guess I better leave you to it." He puts his empty bottle on the table before placing his hand on my shoulder, saying, "Are you sure you want me to email the publishers with your address? You don't want to wait a couple more weeks?"

I shake my head. "I've delayed long enough."

He nods. "I'm off then don't get up. But remember, if you need anything during the week, just text me. Otherwise, I'll see you next weekend."

I go to tell him again that he doesn't have to come down next weekend to check up on me, but we've had the conversation enough times already that I know he insists. Instead, I just say thanks.

I listen for the bang of the front door as he sees himself out, and when it comes, the solitude surrounds me like a warm blanket. For the first time since the accident, I'm truly alone. There is no one around to treat me like I can't do anything for myself, even if it's not far from the truth.

Alone is exactly what I wanted.

SIX

Katie

I can't believe I'm doing this.

Four and a half hours is how long it's taken for me to drive to Cornwall at the whim of a cantankerous fool who has an exaggerated opinion of his own importance to the publishing world. And it's all because coming to London to sign his damn contract *didn't fit into his schedule.*

It doesn't make sense. I read his first gritty, raw bestselling book about his time in Iraq with the Royal Marines. He seemed like a decent guy, but my experience with the man via email is a long way from decent. His never-ending demands are all about what he wants, and too bad if those inconvenience everyone else. I was tempted to just call Mr. A.V. Campbell's bluff and make my own demands.

Come to London to sign the contract or we cancel the deal.

Hunter didn't like that idea. No surprise. He didn't want to risk the author deciding to sign with a more established UK-based publishing house. I get that signing this number one best-selling author ahead of his next release is important but bending to meet some of his more ridiculous demands is crazy.

Nevertheless, here I am, jumping through hoops to personally deliver the paperwork to Mr. A. V. Campbell at his home in Cornwall. Yes, that was one of his demands. He needed me, and only me, to hand deliver his contract to him. What arrogance. Just because I'm the person representing Carlson Publishing and the signatory on his contract doesn't mean I need to physically be there with him when he signs it. Like I don't have anything better to do than run around being his personal courier.

I release a breath full of the frustration I'm feeling. It doesn't help to relieve the knot of tension that has been sitting in my stomach for days, keeping me awake at night. The negotiations on this particular contract have dragged on for a lot longer than they should have. First, Laura, my personal assistant, had to track down the whereabouts of Mr. Campbell, who seemed to drop off the face of the earth a couple of months back. Now here I am trying to find the address his lawyer emailed us last week. A remote little Cornish village where, apparently, the author is on a writing sabbatical. I just want this done, and I guess if I'm the only person who can handle this according to Mr. Campbell, then I'll do it.

I've given myself three days to get the contract signed. Not one day more. I promised Hunter I would have the deal done by the end of the month, and I'm damn well going to. I will be professional and accommodating to any reasonable requests. It's time this farce was over for the sake of my sanity and my team's.

I take another deep breath in and release it slowly this time, easing the tightness in my shoulders. I've been sitting in the car for too long. I'm sure my mood will improve when I can get out and stretch.

Where the hell is this village? I'm sure I was supposed to reach it ten minutes ago. I know, talking to myself in the car doesn't give me the answers I need, but it does help take the edge off my frustration. After all, I don't want to show up on his doorstep appearing angry, because that's bound to trigger some new, equally ridiculous demands.

I pull into a lay-by to check my Google Maps again. Okay, it looks like it's only about another mile to the village where I've made a reservation at the one and only bed-and-breakfast. That's how small this place is. There isn't even a hotel. According to Laura, there's just a small village shop, and of course, a pub. I love the fact that even the tiniest English villages have at least one pub. A place to grab a drink and usually a great meal.

I press the button to wind down the window on my Mercedes-Benz and fill my lungs with the fresh scent of an unseasonably warm spring day. The light breeze blowing across the green fields is earthy, with the faint hint of the nearby sea spray. Maybe being out of the city for a few days won't be so bad after all. This is the first time I've been to this corner of England, and I like it. From what I've seen so far of the county when I've passed through quaint historic towns or caught occasional distant glimpses of the ocean, I'd like to come back and explore more on a vacation.

Reoriented, I start my car and pull out onto the narrow road winding between waist-high, thick hedgerows. The GPS was right; it was only another five minutes to the village and then another ten minutes to the remote cottage.

I pull into the graveled area beside the small white-washed house. This has to be the place since the road stops here, and beyond the barricade is sea cliffs, then ocean as far as you can see.

It feels good to stretch my arms high and work out the kinks in my spine when I step out of the car. Maybe I should have taken more breaks instead of powering through. Birds whirl above me, performing aerial acrobatics from the cliffs, squawking to each other in what I imagine is bird speak for, *Look at what I can do*. This is a ruggedly beautiful place, and now I understand why someone would want to escape here.

With a final deep intake of sea air, I walk carefully through the gravel to the wooden deck. I'm not entirely happy with the damage the tiny stones are likely doing to my Louboutin heels, but my bad. I probably should have worn more sensible shoes. Instead, I was too caught up in the idea of portraying a professional *I mean business* kind of image and these heels make exactly that statement. Well, at least they do when I strut into a boardroom. Out here on a clifftop in Cornwall, maybe not. Oh well, it's too late now. I'm here and eager to get this first meeting with Mr. Campbell over and done with.

The clip-clop of my shoes across the wooden decking sounds loud above the trill of the birds and the distant crash of the waves far below. I'd hoped this announced my arrival, but when I stop at the front door, I don't hear any movement coming from inside. Butterflies take flight in my stomach, a bit like those sea birds, and I tamp them back down with a slow, calming breath in and a shake of my hands. I have no idea what reception I'm going to get.

Rap, rap, rap. The brass knocker is loud when I tap it against the wooden door. At least it should get his attention. I listen again. This time, after a minute, there are distinct shuffling sounds with a different kind of clip-clop approaching.

The door swings open, and I step back, my mouth dropping open fully.

It takes a moment for my vocal cords to work, and I squeak out, "Drew?" A name I never expected to utter again. Not after my one-night stand from months ago disappeared before I woke the next morning without even a goodbye.

I've struggled to forget the mysterious Scotsman who rocked my world multiple times. How can I, when it's his face, his hands, and his body I imagine in my dreams or when my magic wand is bringing me to orgasm?

But all that aside, why would Drew be here? Where is Mr. Campbell? Nothing makes sense to my muddled brain, which is firing questions, none of which are spoken.

Instead, I end up saying, "What the hell are you doing here?" My voice is harsh, unfiltered by politeness. I can hear my mother's voice in my head telling me, *There is no need for that tone.*

I shake her voice back into the recesses of my brain. There is every reason for me to be angry this time. This is the guy who snuck away while I slept, like a thief in the night stealing my orgasms.

My eyes travel quickly from his dripping wet hair to his damp bare chest and down to the low-slung black sweatpants hooked on his lean hips. A large white towel in his hand indicates that I've interrupted his shower. I drag my gaze back to his face, and a smirk teases the corners of his lips as he swipes the towel over his hair. Memories of the talented things that mouth could do spring to mind.

Realizing my own mouth is now hanging open, I quickly close it. He knows I was checking him out and almost drooling over the sight of his half-naked body. But I'm not about to let that distract me. He leans casually against the doorframe, and I know he's not surprised at all to see me. I've been set up, and I don't like it.

With a shake of my head, I recover enough to confidently demand, "Why are you here?" in the voice I use to address the boardroom.

His mouth ticks up into a full smug smile as he replies simply, "I live here."

I'm not amused by his flippant response, and I push for more. "But this is where the author A.V. Campbell lives." My brain is struggling to put all the facts together.

Drew tilts his head, left, then right before holding out his hand to me and saying, "Aye, I'm Andrew Vincent Campbell." I ignore his outstretched hand, and he drops it, then shrugs his shoulders. "Would you like to come in, Ms. Carlson?"

Huh, so he does know exactly who I am. It's all beginning to make sense, and he's got some explaining to do.

I can't believe he has deliberately deceived me into coming all this way. Why?

At least I get why he would never accept my calls, because I absolutely would have recognized his voice. How could I forget the sound of his deep, sexy growl when he whispered dirty words into the shell of my ear?

To say I'm angry would be a gross understatement. I'm foot-stomping, steam-coming-out-my-ears furious. And filled with so many questions that I can't settle on the first one to ask.

Instead, I stomp into the room, spin on my heels, and with hands on my hips blurt out, "You lied to me."

"Sorry," he says before turning his back on me and moving in an awkward shuffle the short distance over to a set of open doors at the end of the room. I stare at his back and another question forms. *What's wrong with him?* He no longer seems to move in the swift, athletic way I remember from our night together.

Brushing the thought aside, I follow him, not happy that he dared to walk away from me before I've had my say.

"Hey, buddy. I haven't finished. In fact, I haven't even started with what I have to say."

He stands statue still in the open doorway, his back to me. It's like he didn't even hear me. I move to stand beside him.

"Are you going to say anything? Like maybe explain to me why the hell you felt the need to lie to get me here at literally the end of the country? And more importantly, why now, months after we met?" I look down at his arm where my finger is poking him. I didn't even realize I'd been waving it at him, and now it's pressing on his warm, firm skin.

I pull it back sharply and suck in several deep breaths, trying to calm myself and quell the rapid beating of my heart. Just standing next to this man has me jittery and flustered. I tell myself that *it's just anger.*

He turns to face me. "Hold that thought." He drops his towel on the back of a nearby chair and picks up the T-shirt draped over it. Good, his bare chest is distracting.

My mouth drops open, my fists clench at my sides, and I only just stop myself from screaming out my frustration at his nonchalant demeanor. I'm imploding. But before I can gather my fury to fire back a response, he shrugs the fabric down over his head, then places his hands on my upper arms.

I feel the heat from his body as he leans in close to whisper in my ear. "Katie, I'm truly sorry."

I step back from his gentle hold and glare at him. "Please, don't touch me. All I need from you right now are words. Nothing more."

He nods once, turns, then steps cautiously through the door.

My eyes drift down to check out his ass, and I wish I hadn't. I don't need a reminder of how good his butt looks. My memory from two months ago hasn't diminished.

I step through the doors after him, determined to get an answer to my most burning question: *Why did he leave that night?* I've had this rattling around in my head for long enough. But first I need the bathroom. My bladder is bursting, and I need a moment to process seeing Drew again.

"Could I use your bathroom?"

He looks over his shoulder at me, his brows raised like it's a trick question. "Sure, it's through the kitchen." He points back into the cottage, and I walk back inside to find a large modern bathroom at the back of the cottage.

I'd hoped slipping away would give me a few minutes to recover from the feel of his hands on my arms. A simple touch that sucked the fight right out of me and replaced it with a desperate need to escape. Turns out the bathroom isn't the temporary refuge I thought it would be. The space wraps me in an intoxicating Drew-filled haze, from the fresh lime scent of his shower gel to the masculine woodsy cologne I remember clearly from our night together.

When I woke up the morning after the awards party to an empty bed, I was more than disappointed. It hurt. I know it was only meant to be a one-night stand, but the connection between us felt like so much more. What Drew could do to me and the fevered heights of pleasure he transported me to were unique and special. He obviously didn't feel the same, otherwise he would have stayed till morning.

It's my fault for reading too much into our one-night stand. He never promised anything more than some fun sexy times, so I shouldn't have come away feeling disillusioned. Never again. I'm not a one-night stand kind of girl.

Anyway, that was months ago, and I've moved on. Although I haven't dated or slept with another guy since, I've moved on enough that I didn't expect to see Drew again.

Yet here he is. Where he has always been. Hiding in plain sight this whole time. Biding his time till he decided he wanted to let me know who he really was. I think back to all those back-and-forth emails between us these last couple of weeks, and a fresh bout of anger washes over me.

I quickly freshen up and return to the living area, walking through the open doors and out onto the small wooden deck overlooking the sea. Drew is lounging casually in a deck chair, his legs stretched out straight and ankles crossed loosely in front of him. A jug of water and two glasses sit on the table beside him. At least out here I can only smell the salty sea breeze and not him.

"Katie, I'd like to explain everything if you'll let me. Please."

His hand gestures toward the other deck chair. I sit, perching on the edge of it.

When I'm settled, he asks, "Would you like some water?" I nod. I'm thrown by the conventionality of the question and watch on while he fills both glasses. He hands me the frosted glass of water, and I take it, avoiding his touch.

The icy liquid soothes my raw throat. Then, placing the glass back on the table, I look out toward the sea and wait. Drew's the one who needs to do the talking, and I'm not about to make it easier for him by starting us off.

He releases a sigh. "All right, let's start at the night of the party."

My eyes dart back to him. "Yes, let's," I say with a scathing edge to my voice, then sit back in the chair with my arms folded around my body and my legs crossed.

He sits up straighter, and I turn away again to stare, unseeing, at the deep blue expanse below, the sound of waves crashing up against the rocks at the base of the cliff an apt backdrop to the way I'm feeling.

"Katie, I had every intention of staying that night and waking up next to you. But when I went to get us some water early that morning, I saw your pass and realized who you were."

I look sideways at him, and he runs his hand roughly through his hair. It's longer than I remember it.

He glances at me, then quickly looks back out to sea before continuing. "I was worried that our night together would jeopardize the contract negotiations. We had nearly reached a deal, and I guess I panicked. It was stupid, really." He seems to struggle with the words. I get the impression that he doesn't often have to apologize for doing stupid things.

He turns back to me, and this time holds my gaze as he says, "Katie, I'm sorry I took off rather than staying and explaining who I was. I regret leaving for that and many more reasons."

His voice dips low, and there's a somber quality about it. His head is bent, looking down at his legs.

"Fine. I get that you're sorry and all that. But it was two months ago. You've known all that time who I am, and yet only now are you deciding to inform me. Why now and why like this?"

I'm not letting him get away with a simple sorry, no matter how heartfelt it sounds.

He scrubs both hands across his eyes so roughly it's like he's trying to erase something. "Well, there's a reason. In my rush to leave that morning, I called a minicab to take me back to my friend's house where I was staying." His voice drops lower, and I strain to hear the next words. "On the way, there was an accident. A drunk driver slammed into the front of us. My minicab driver and the guy driving the other car were both killed instantly, and I was injured."

I gasp.

A flash of pain transforms his features before he continues in the same low, dull voice. "I woke up in hospital a couple of days later pretty smashed up."

I reach out to rest my hand on his arm. "Are you okay?"

He looks down at where I'm touching him, then back up into my eyes. "Mostly, but it will be a while still before I'm back to walking normally, if ever. I've spent the last two months trying to heal my broken body. My legs bore the brunt of the impact."

I feel bad for my earlier accusations, although I would never have imagined a horrific accident was the reason. I withdraw my hand, and he leans forward in his chair, his hands clasped between his knees. He appears to be deep in thought.

I'm compelled to fill the silence. "That sounds terrible. Do you remember much about the accident?"

He shakes his head. "Not really. More just the flash of lights and the smell of gasoline. I've been told since that I was pinned in the wreckage for a couple of hours until they could pry the metal off me.

I'm glad I don't remember that."

"Oh, Drew. I'm sorry."

He sighs like he's heard the platitude before. "I'm lucky to be alive and have the function of my legs. I'm grateful for that. The minicab driver didn't get that chance." I nod. It's so sad that the driver died because of a stupid, irresponsible act.

Again, I reach out to rest my palm on the warm skin of his forearm. It's a small comfort when it's obvious he's still coming to terms with the accident.

I guess I knew there was something different about Drew when I first saw him. But I was so caught up with my own hurt and anger that it didn't really sink in. I look more closely at him, and it's now obvious that he's leaner in the face. In fact, he appears to have lost weight all over. I'm a terrible person for being too busy checking out his ass to notice the changes in him.

"I'm sorry I jumped down your throat the moment I walked in the door. I should have let you explain."

"No, you had every right to be angry. I snuck out while you were sleeping. And on the surface, I looked like an arsehole." He offers me a small smile.

"How are you recovering then?"

"I'm doing better than the doctors expected. And in a couple of weeks, I might even get an all clear to be able to drive again. That was why I couldn't meet you in London."

"Of course. How do you get around then?" I ask. I should have noticed when I parked outside that there wasn't another car here.

He attempts a smile, but it doesn't quite reach his eyes. Another change in him I didn't notice initially. "I get dinner delivered from the local pub a couple of times a week. Other than that, it's what I brought with me and what my friend Aaron brings when he visits on the weekends."

"Why on earth did you choose to stay in this isolated cottage?

Surely you could have gotten something in a village or town."

This time, his smile is broader. "I like the isolation. I was sick of having people around me constantly in the hospital and rehabilitation center. As soon as Aaron could spring me, he did. I hated being monitored twenty-four seven."

I frown at him. "But maybe that was for your own good. I'm sure they had the best of intentions."

"Aye, I agree. I just don't make a very good patient." He stretches back in the chair, shuffling his legs awkwardly, no longer trying to hide his injuries from me. I remove my hand from his arm, only then realizing it had been resting there this whole time. He looks sideways at me with one brow arched.

I pick up my glass of water, pretending that was the reason I removed my hand. I take a sip, then place it back on the table.

"How are your legs now?" I ask, wanting to understand his steps to recovery better.

"Slow, and apart from them being held together with a ridiculous amount of metal, most days, they're okay. It took a while to learn to walk again. I only need to use the crutches around the cottage some days or when I'm outside on rough ground, which I try to avoid."

I can't believe he's chosen to isolate himself on this clifftop with no one around to help him. It seems like a crazy idea to me, but I keep my opinion to myself.

I glance down at my watch and see it's getting late. "I better be going. I still need to check into the bed-and-breakfast in the village before it gets late and they decide to give my room away to someone else."

He coughs out a laugh. "Unlikely. They don't get a lot of visitors passing through, even in the summer months."

"Good point. But still, I should get going." I stand up. "Is there anything you need?"

He appears to consider my question before saying, "Aye, there is. You could pick up dinner from the pub and bring it back to eat with me." I look down at where he's still seated in the chair. Was this his plan all along?

I had thought it would be good to have some time to let everything that Drew just told me sink in. But now I can't really refuse to help after just offering.

I plaster a smile on my face and reply, "Sure, I can do that." Then, glancing down at my watch again, I continue, "Is seven o'clock okay?" That should give me a couple of hours to gather my defenses.

Drew pulls himself to standing beside me, and again, I can't believe I missed earlier how stiffly and cautiously he moves. I take a step back out of the danger zone that is Drew's personal space.

"Um, text me your dinner order. You have my number." I don't even try to mask the edge to my voice. Drew still has a lot more explaining to do. I continue to back away from him, wanting to leave quickly and escape any awkward goodbyes. "I'll see you at seven. I can see myself out."

Luckily, he doesn't say more other than a brief "see you later."

Back in my car, I grip the steering wheel with both hands and rest my head on them. I'm feeling overwhelmed by everything Drew just shared. Never in a million years could I have imagined that a serious accident was the reason he didn't contact me. Not that I even knew he had my name.

There is a lot to unpack, but right now, I have to get checked into my room. The thought of a long, hot shower washing away the travel grime has me turning on my car and pulling away from the cottage.

SEVEN

Drew

That went better than I thought it would, I tell myself as I drop back into the deck chair and gently stretch out my legs. Sharp pain shoots up my right leg, radiating throughout my body. My eyes squeeze shut, and I grit my teeth until the muscle spasm eases. I'm suffering for choosing to fake it in front of Katie earlier.

It was stupid pride that had me attempting to walk without limping. I've put too much weight on my more severely injured right leg and will have to suffer the consequences now. I didn't want to display any weakness in front of her when the truth is I can barely walk without crutches.

I dig my fingers into my right thigh, hoping to ease the

muscles that are tightly knotted. I'll take some of the stronger pain medication the doctor gave me just before Katie returns with our takeout so I can make it through dinner. And then tomorrow morning, I'll need to book an appointment for my physio, Sean, who lives in the neighboring village, to make a special trip out to work on me. Physical therapy is a new form of torture that I don't think I'll ever get accustomed to. No matter how much better it feels an hour after he finishes. I swear Sean has knives in his fingertips when he manipulates the muscles in my lower back, thighs, and calves. Almost as bad will be the rant he'll launch into throughout the treatment. He's bound to have plenty to say about me pushing too hard with my recovery.

I've come a long way since I finally woke up in the hospital days after the accident, but still, my recovery is not fast enough for me. It's frustratingly slow building back my strength after having to spend seven weeks in a wheelchair. Knowing it could have been a lifetime gives me pause.

The bone in my left leg was broken in one place and only needed a cast. What the doctors referred to as a closed fracture. It was the right leg that was crushed and mangled in the wreckage. Once some of the swelling had gone down, the doctors operated to realign the bone fragments properly. They implanted plates, rods, and screws to hold the bones in the proper position. During those initial weeks, a metal frame was attached to the outside of my leg with pins anchoring it to my bone. The worst part was not being able to move from the bed. I don't like sitting still, and it nearly drove me insane. At least it worked, and when the Frankenstein-like device was removed seven weeks later, I could walk. Maybe more of a shuffle with a frame and not strictly the act of walking, but I was upright, and the long rehabilitation process could truly begin.

Stupidly, I thought rehab would only be a couple of weeks. I was wrong.

***

Exactly at seven, a soft knock on the door announces Katie's return. I shout out to come in as I continue my pathetically slow efforts of pulling plates, cutlery, and glasses from the cupboards in the kitchen. Tonight, there's no point in trying to hide my injuries because, even with the pain medication, I can barely move.

I turn around, and she's standing in the doorway of the kitchen. A drop-dead gorgeous woman who appears completely at odds with the simple surroundings of the cabin. Luckily, I'm already holding on to the countertop, or my weak legs may have crumpled pathetically under me.

I've seen party-girl Katie at the awards night, then corporate boss lady Katie earlier today, but this version of Katie is, I think, my new favorite. She's dressed casually in tight-fitting black jeans with a light cream woolen top that has slipped teasingly off one finely boned shoulder. I remember kissing her on that shoulder months ago, and I wish we were at a point where I could do that tonight. But I suspect that if I tried it, I'd earn myself a well-deserved slap or punch.

I recover my equilibrium enough to say, "Hey, you don't need to knock when you visit. You can come straight in. I don't lock my door, and it can take me a while to get to it, like earlier today."

She nods. "Where would you like me to put the food?" The smell of hot fish and chips fills the tiny kitchen and has my mouth watering.

"Take it directly out to the deck if you like. I thought we could eat out there if that's okay with you."

With a murmured "Perfect," she turns and walks toward the open double doors. I briefly watch the sway of her hips before reclaiming my crutches, which are leaning against the wall beside me. Then, picking up the handles of the bag I packed the plates and things into, I begin the tediously slow hobble across the room.

I've only made it halfway when Katie comes back through the doors and rushes over to me. "Let me get that for you." Before I can say anything, she takes the bag from my fingers and heads back outside.

She may have thought she hid the look of surprise from me, but she didn't. I grit my teeth over the expletives that are fighting up my throat and wanting to be expelled. It's not her fault that my body has become useless. I need to get over my shit.

Maybe I should have waited until I could walk properly before manipulating events to get her to drive all the way to Cornwall to see me. Not one of my best ideas.

It was a selfish dick move tricking Katie by not telling her who I was. I briefly considered calling or emailing her, but I suspect I wouldn't have gotten past her PA. This is personal, and the last thing I wanted was to risk someone on her staff reading something they shouldn't. I needed to explain the situation in person, and given my limited mobility, I couldn't just walk into her office. Currently, I can't fucking walk the few steps to the doorway unaided. My crutch hits the leg of the desk chair, and I step down hard on my right leg. Fuck, that hurt.

I take a deep breath, sucking up the pain. Then, on the exhale, I push forward on my crutches to join Katie on the deck. By the time I've clumsily maneuvered into the deck chair, she has already laid out the plates and is putting a serving of battered fish and crispy golden chips on each of them.

"Hmm, this does smell good," she exclaims while she dishes up the meal, and I wish I could muster up the same enthusiasm. My mood is soured, partly by the pain still shooting up my right leg and partly because of this feeling of pathetic helplessness.

"What would you like to drink?" she asks. "I do have a bottle of wine."

"No, that's the last thing I need with the medication I took earlier," I grumble.

She straightens in her chair, her eyes wide. "I'll grab us some water, then." And she jumps up, rushing back inside. It's like she's looking for any excuse to not be in my company. Who could blame her?

Fuck, I'm an asshole. This meal is not turning out the way I wanted it to. I don't know what I was expecting when I can barely get myself out of bed, showered, and changed these days. It's not surprising that I can't treat Katie to a nice meal. No, I have to sit here instead, having her run around after me all night.

Katie returns with two tall glasses of water and places them on the table between us.

I reach for her hand before she can find another reason to run off. "Katie, I'm sorry. I'm not very good company tonight." She stares down at where I'm touching her, then back up at me.

"Do you want me to leave?"

"No, not at all. I just wanted to apologize for growling at you."

She smiles sweetly at me. "Funny. I remember your growling being very different."

I throw my head back and laugh. In the blink of an eye, or really, one short quip, she has brushed aside my bad mood. Maybe having her here in my domain was a good idea after all. It's allowed me the chance to apologize and explain what happened while also removing any awkwardness from our future business discussions.

Smiling, she looks down at the meal and says, "Come on, let's eat before it gets cold. This looks delicious, and I'm hungry."

"Good idea." I reach for a sachet of malt vinegar, then offer her one. "Do you want vinegar on your chips?"

She looks at me oddly. "Why would I want to put vinegar on my chips?"

"It's braw."

She laughs. "Have I mentioned that sometimes I have no idea

what you're saying? What is braw?" She wrinkles her nose cutely when she pronounces the word, and I laugh along with her.

"It means great, fantastic. What I was saying was vinegar on chips tastes great. Do you want to try it? It's a British tradition."

"Ah … No thanks, but do you have mayo?"

I shake my head, smiling at the easy, light banter. It's nice to not be thinking about the accident or my injuries. They've been the focus of the last two months—every discussion and every thought. I'm over it.

We settle into a comfortable conversation while we eat our simple meal. It's an easy sharing of thoughts from favorite foods to places we've traveled.

***

The next morning, Sean digs his thumbs into the back of my right thigh. I'm lying facedown on the portable therapy table in the middle of the living room, my face pushed hard into the hole and my fists gripping so tightly to the sides of the table my knuckles have turned a ghostly white.

Sean chuckles. "Hang in there, mate. I'm nearly done. Just a few more minutes." Sean is a big Australian dude who could probably become a good friend if he wasn't also my sadistic torturer. He calls himself a physical therapist, and when he uses acupuncture to ease my pain, I'd be willing to call him that too. But on days like today, when he does these hard muscle manipulation sessions that are the thing of nightmares, I want to fucking beat him to a pulp.

He hits a particularly painful knot of muscle, and I can't hold back a pained groan. "That fucking hurts like a bitch," I complain loudly, and he has the nerve to chuckle. I grit my teeth and brace for more pain.

It's then that the front door squeaks open, and the click of heels on the wooden floorboards give me only a second's warning before Katie says, "Oh, excuse me. Um, sorry. I can wait outside. I didn't realize you were … busy."

I can't lift my head to see her, but I can imagine the pink blush on her cheeks.

Sean's hands are no longer inflicting pain, so I'm grateful for the timely interruption. "Katie, this is Sean, my physio," I mumble through the gap in the table before hearing them greet each other. "We're nearly finished. Aren't we, Sean?" I threaten, then grit my teeth as his thumbs return to hit the same painful spot again. I visibly flinch.

"Still, I'll wait on the deck till you're finished." I catch a glimpse of red heels as she walks by, and I'm tempted to lift my head to see what version of Katie I have today. I suspect, based on the shoes, that we're back to boss lady, which means she's here for business. It's a shame that her idea of business is not the kind I'd like to be doing with her.

After a very enjoyable dinner together last night, I'm rethinking my stance on keeping my hands off her. Business never mixes well with pleasure. But thoughts of the beautiful woman kept me awake last night and into the early hours of this morning.

Maybe a repeat of our one-night stand wouldn't be such a bad idea.

Sean finishes up with a few more sharp pokes and prods, then helps me to standing. I wrap the large white towel around my waist and watch as he quickly packs up his gear. Then, with a cheerful promise to return in two days, he leaves. The dude seems to get way too much pleasure out of inflicting pain on me.

Unsteadily, I make my way slowly over to the glass doors, leaning heavily on furniture and walls where I can. It already feels like I'm moving more freely than I was at the start of the day, but that's still no better than an octogenarian. My legs are sore and shaky, and I brace my arms against the doorframe leading out to the deck.

Outside, Katie is standing at the edge of the deck, looking out at the ocean. It's a sunny but breezy day with the deep blue expanse chopped up and dotted with whitecaps. The sound of the waves hitting the rocks is louder, and the air is filled with a salty sea spray. I love these wilder days better than the calm ones. They just have a way of making you feel glad to be alive. And even in my weakened state, I'm glad to be here in this moment, gazing at the back of the truly stunning woman before me.

I quietly admire her kick-ass stance, one hand on her hip, the other holding back a swathe of dark hair from being blown about in the blustery wind. My eyes briefly trail down her body from her narrow waist that flares out into curvy hips to the sweetest peachy butt all encased in her tight black skirt. Then there are those long, shapely legs that end in a pair of traffic-stopping red shoes that should not turn me on but do.

I quickly adjust myself through the thick towel so my admiration is not so embarrassingly obvious, then clear my throat.

"Hey, I'm done." She jumps slightly at the sound of my voice. Obviously, her thoughts were a million miles away. "Sorry, I didn't mean to startle you," I say when she turns to face me.

She shakes her head. "No, you didn't." Her gaze is laser focused on my eyes. It seems odd until I realize that she's trying not to look at the towel knotted low on my hips. Now that's a boost to the ego.

I rub my hand across my chest several times. "Geez, today's session was brutal. Sorry we were running a bit late, but Sean was held up with an earlier patient."

Katie's eyes are now tracking the movement of my hand, and if I had to guess from her heated gaze, she's wishing it was her hand.

"No … no, really, it's all good."

Knowing that she's interested has me going back to my earlier thoughts. I wonder if she'd like to hop back into my bed. And before the idea is even completely formed, I ask, "Katie, could you help me into the bedroom? Those sessions leave me weak, and I don't want to stumble."

Her eyes go saucer wide. "Um, okay." She moves to stand beside me, and I hook my arm over her shoulders. Her arm slides tentatively around my waist, her hand coming to rest on my bare skin just above the towel.

Forced proximity is another asshole move on my part, but I don't care. I'm holding her close for the first time since our night together, and even if it's purely as an aid rather than sexual, it feels really good. Her sweet fruity perfume is tantalizing, but it's the feel of her silky hair brushing against my chest that has me grinning from ear to ear.

She carefully shuffles me across the room. Maybe I didn't need to lean so heavily on her, and maybe I could have moved faster. But she feels so good. I want to drag out this moment and remember what we were like together that night. This may be all I get.

As we reach the doorway to the galley kitchen, there really isn't any need for her to help me anymore, because the space between the countertop on one side and the wall on the other wouldn't allow us to pass through shoulder to shoulder.

I lean back against the end of the counter, my arm still hooked loosely around her. "Thanks. I think I've got it from here."

With a slight tilt of my head, I touch my lips to her cheek in a casual, friendly kiss that is anything but casual when the touch lasts longer than it should.

I hear her sharp intake of breath and the slow release of air when I remove my lips. She hasn't forgotten that night, just like I haven't. I didn't expect a repeat of our hookup in the hotel room when I coerced her into coming to Cornwall. Really, all I wanted to do was apologize and set the record straight. But now that she's here, her perfume teasing my nostrils, my hands wanting to run through her dark glossy hair, and her chocolate brown eyes looking at me with melting desire, I'm reminded of why I was initially attracted to her. She's hard to resist.

But I do, for now.

I walk the five steps to the end of the kitchen, and even though I have my back to her, I feel her eyes on me. With one hand on the door to the bedroom, I loosen the towel at my waist with the other, giving her an eyeful of my bare butt.

EIGHT

Katie

Don't look, I tell myself, but I still continue to stare hungrily at Drew's naked body.

What a jerk, letting the towel drop and flashing me his sexy butt. He knows how much I liked checking out his perfect, firmly muscled glutes when he stripped in the hotel room. His body may be leaner than it was back then due to the accident, but one fleeting glance has the ability to make me want him all over again.

Finally finding my voice, I shout after him, "That is so juvenile." His only response is a deep, rumbling chuckle before the bang of the door he just disappeared through. Well, if he thinks his little stunt will have me following him, he is so wrong. I still need more answers before I intend to go anywhere near that temptation.

Wait, what am I thinking? I have no intention of jumping into bed with him again. Sure, our one night was spectacularly memorable. But that's also the reason why I should avoid a repeat. Drew has the potential to set the bar so high no other guy in my future stands a chance.

I turn and flop down into the single chair in the living room and promptly sink into its cushioned softness. Pure indulgence. I could do with a chair like this for my home office.

The distant sound of the shower being turned on has me pulling out my phone to scroll through emails. The perfect distraction from thoughts of Drew in the shower, water cascading down his naked body. I recross my legs. Thinking sexy thoughts about Drew is not going to get the contract signed. Last night, as I lay in bed unable to sleep, my mind replaying Drew's accident, our one-night stand, and the reason I'm here in Cornwall, I made a decision. Today, I need to get back to business.

Twenty minutes later, Drew clomps back through the doorway on his crutches wearing gray sweats and a fitted black T-shirt. Oh please, he has to be taunting me now. Everyone knows that gray sweats are a complete turn-on when worn by a guy with a body like Drew's, all lean, sinewy muscle. I'd bet anything that he's commando underneath them too. Damn him.

I hold back the groan wanting to spill from my lips and instead, roll my eyes at him before looking back down at my phone. The metallic clip-clop of the crutches on the wooden floor as he advances closer to me makes the phone in my hand wobble, and I place it facedown on my lap and look up. He stares down at me, smirking. Yes, he knows exactly what he's doing.

He might think he can play me like a puppet, but he knows nothing if he thinks I'm going to sit here meekly and mildly, just looking while he flashes his butt at me or jiggles his semihard cock around in gray sweats. Uncrossing my legs, I stand to bring myself not to his height but certainly at less of a height disadvantage.

Two can play his game.

"So, are you going to tell me what the hell this is?" I wave my hand between us. We stand toe to toe. I realize too late it's a mistake to stand this close to him. I release a breath, which at some point turned from annoyed into turned-on.

He tilts his head to the side, and his smile has an *I knew you couldn't resist me* vibe about it. Why am I hopeless at hiding my thoughts from him? It's annoying that he seems to be able to read me so easily.

Catching me completely by surprise, he smashes his lips to mine. It's a hot, wet kiss that makes my knees wobble. His tongue slips between my parted lips. I offer no resistance. I let him take my breath away. But just as quickly as the kiss escalates, he stops. My head is spinning. I stare at him. He rubs a hand across his eyes, then looks away.

With a frustrated huff, I brush past him, striding into his kitchen with an extra sway to my hips. I help myself to a glass of water, trying to erase the taste of his tongue on mine. It gives me a moment to think, even though I know he's watching my every move. I refill my glass, then return.

"It's time we talked business," I tell him in my most professional-sounding tone. He nods, the earlier smile erased from his mouth as he moves over to the two-seater sofa. I place my glass of water on the coffee table and resume my seat opposite him.

He maneuvers his body slowly onto the sofa, resting his crutches against the armrest, then says, "Fine, what business are you wanting to discuss, Ms. Carlson?"

"Your contract. The whole reason you tricked me into coming down here. Oh, and don't think we've finished that conversation either." I promised Hunter I could do this, and I'm damn well going to. I refuse to let Drew distract me with hot, steamy kisses or tempting displays of his sexy body.

He nods. I take that as acknowledgement of my statement that we're not done, but also that he's willing to talk business.

He leans forward on the sofa. "Did you receive the amendments sent through last month?" he asks, and a sigh of relief escapes from my lungs. Finally, he's taking me seriously.

I fish out a bundle of papers from my leather tote. "Yes, and this is a copy of the contract with those amendments your lawyer requested. It's a copy of the electronic version we sent you on the twentieth. Have you had a chance to read that?"

"No, sorry. I've been a bit busy." His voice is low and flat.

Damn it, he couldn't possibly have read it when he was laid up in a hospital bed after being put back together by a group of doctors.

"Yes, of course. I can leave this copy with you to read overnight. We can discuss it further tomorrow. But really, I don't have a lot of time to finalize this, so I would appreciate a quick turnaround."

He stares at me like I've just grown two heads. Maybe it has something to do with the way I just laid out the timeline, because even to my own ears, I sound cold and robotic. I don't know what's wrong with me. Usually, I'm so much nicer when I'm discussing contracts with authors. But then I've never slept with an author I've been negotiating with before either.

I drop the pages on the coffee table between us, then release a heavy sigh. "Sorry, I'm having trouble compartmentalizing. It's difficult to see you as A.V. Campbell, the author I'm conducting contract negotiations with, when, on the other hand, you're Drew, the man I had hot, raunchy sex with a couple of months ago."

He rests his forearms on his knees and clasps his hands in front. This, I'm learning, is his thinking position. I wait, and after about a minute, he says, "If it helps, I'm struggling with this too. Look, I promise I'll read the updated contract and discuss it with my lawyer overnight. We should be ready to finalize it all tomorrow."

My smile this time comes more readily. "Thank you, I appreciate that." I relax back into my chair, happy that we seem to be making progress—with the contract at least. My attraction to the man, though, remains a problem.

When the silence begins to stretch uncomfortably between us, I look around the room, my eyes snagging on the closed laptop on the desk in the corner.

"How is the writing going? It can't have been easy with the accident and everything." I look back at Drew, and he's staring blankly at the desk. "Are you okay?"

He turns to face me again. "Aye. I don't like talking about my work in progress, but don't worry, I'll make the deadline." His voice is uncharacteristically angry, and I can't fathom what I said that upset him.

"Drew, I wasn't asking about the deadline. I was only asking if everything was okay." I pick up my glass of water and take a sip to hide my confusion. He is a lot moodier than I remember.

His eyes bore into me, and my stomach flips under the intensity of his stare. "I'm fine," he says, and his fingers begin to drum a silent, steady rhythm on his left knee. I wish I could read him as easily as he does me.

Maybe now is as good a time as any to ask another of the questions I've had since I arrived on his doorstep. There's already a tension in the air, and I've never been someone to back away from the hard stuff.

I sit up straighter and return his stare. "Why did you insist I come down here personally to deliver the contracts? We could have done this via email."

The finger tapping stops. "I wanted to see you again to apologize. In person." His expression is still completely unreadable.

I release the breath I was holding and push for more. "Why?"

The corners of his mouth tick up slightly. "Because, even with everything that happened to me, I couldn't get that night out of my head. I felt bad for taking off. You didn't deserve that."

His honesty in admitting that our night was special goes a long way to melting the ball of anger and hurt I felt when I woke up and he was gone. But I need more.

"You knew who I was. It was always inevitable that we would see each other again."

"Aye, it was always going to be awkward. Katie, I didn't want to wait and … I didn't want our next meeting to be across a conference table."

This time my "Why?" is more of a whispered plea. His heated gaze is confusing the messages firing in my brain and making it impossible to remain unmoved.

He draws in a deep breath and slowly releases it again. "Because … I want a repeat of that night."

"What?" I choke out before slumping lower into the chair. It's lucky I was already sitting, because I'm sure his statement would have floored me.

His unflinching stormy gray gaze holds me frozen in place. "Katie, I didn't plan this. But I've realized now that you're here that I want to taste you on my tongue and hear your moans again. Just like that night, I want to fuck you so hard, so completely, you won't know where I end and you begin." My mouth drops open. This is what I imagined he was saying to me in my dreams last night and a few other times over the last two months.

Shit. No one has ever spoken to me like that before, and it's the hottest thing I've ever heard. My whole body is pulsing with need. My panties are damp at the thought of all those delicious things he just outlined. I want everything he just said … and more. But I pull myself up on those thoughts. Just because I dreamed of him saying these things doesn't mean I should make them a reality.

"Do you always get what you want?" I challenge before running my tongue over my suddenly dry lips.

"You fuckin' better believe it. Will you come over here?" he growls, the throaty sound melting my defenses further.

Surprising him but also myself, I stand on shaky legs, take a step toward him, then stop. "This feels like a bad idea."

"Aye, but you want this as badly as I do. I can see it in your eyes. We were too good together for just one night."

He holds my gaze, and like he's some kind of snake charmer, his softly spoken words draw me to him. I tentatively take the remaining three steps to close the distance between us. He leans back into the sofa, looking up at me, and for the first time, I notice the impressive bulge tenting his gray sweats. He's right. I do want his body again, and I reach down to touch him.

But he grabs me by the wrist, restraining me in a viselike grip. "First, I want you to strip for me," he demands in a gravelly tone that I haven't heard before. It's sexy, compelling, and forceful. I never thought I'd want to bend to a man's will, but with Drew, I want to hand over complete control. Especially when I know what delicious things he can do with that control.

I bend to remove my red patent leather Jimmy Choo heels, and in the same voice, Drew tells me, "Leave those on."

I look up, standing up straight again, then begin to undo the buttons on the front of my white silk blouse. His heated gaze tracks my progress.

"Good girl," he encourages, and I feel my cheeks flush under his praise.

When the last button is undone, I slip it from my shoulders and let it flutter to the floor behind me. His eyes darken as he takes in my lacy white bra, then he mutters, "Beautiful."

Never before have I been as glad to have a thing for pretty lingerie. My drawers at home are overflowing with sexy sets of expensive underwear in every color imaginable. Choosing a set to wear each day is as important to me as choosing the clothes to go on top. A small smile reaches my lips as I think of Drew's reaction when he catches sight of the matching G-string still hidden under my skirt.

I reach around behind me to unhook, then unzip my simple black skirt, shimmying it down over my hips until it too falls to the floor. I take a step sideways out of it. Feeling cheeky, I turn and bend deeply, picking up my skirt and tossing it across to the other chair.

Drew groans loudly. "Fuuuck me." Still bent over with my bare butt in his face, I peer over my shoulder, grinning. His mouth is hanging open, his eyes are wide, and his cock is out of his sweats and in his fist. Seeing him enjoying himself gives me an extra boost of confidence. I stand, then spin around on slightly wobbly legs to face him. He looks at me hungrily, his fist sliding slowly up and then down his shaft.

"Don't stop. Pretty as your lacy underwear is, I want it all off," he demands again.

Before today, I never would have thought I could be a submissive, yet here I am, doing everything this man demands of me and doing it willingly, eagerly. With a stretch of my arm, I reach behind me to unclip my bra and throw it somewhere behind me, then I slide the G-string down my legs.

When it's at my feet, Drew holds out his hand. "Give me them."

I slip the panties over my shoes and place them on his palm. His fingers close tightly over them, and he brings his fist to his nose, breathing in deeply. I've never seen a guy do that before. I didn't even know that was a thing. It feels naughty in an erotic kind of way, making me feel totally desirable.

I take one step forward and drop to my knees before him, then place my hand over his and whisper, "Please may I?" He drops his hand, and I curl my fingers around the base of his thick, firm shaft.

I'd be worried about the stretch if I didn't already know that we fit together perfectly. His member is larger than any other guy I've been with. Not that the five other sexual partners from my past are much of a sample.

I lean forward, knowing that this position will make my nipples brush against his knees. I lick across the tip. His salty precum hits my tastebuds, and my core aches with desire. I want more, and I seal my lips around his crown, then look up at him. He groans low and deep.

Another couple of teasing swipes of my tongue, and he threads the fingers of both hands through my hair. His grip is tight as he firmly holds me to him. Emboldened, I take in more, stuffing my mouth with his cock, loving the feel of him hitting the back of my throat.

I slowly draw back. He pulses his hips forward, and I suck him in again, sheathing my teeth with my lips so he feels the pressure along his shaft. With my tongue flattened and pressing firmly to the underside of his length, I relax my throat muscles and take him in farther. My eyes water, and I tamp down on my gag reflex.

His breathing is coming in fast, short pants, and it drives me on to push him to the brink. I bob my head up and down on him a few more times until he tugs back hard on my hair.

"Fuck, Katie, that's enough," he growls.

I look up at him, wide-eyed, then back down at his tempting, impressive thick shaft, standing up proudly and smeared in my long-lasting Gucci rose lipstick. I smile.

He reaches out and rubs his thumb over my bottom lip. "You really like sucking cock, don't you, baby?"

I nod vigorously, because I really do. Especially his.

He reaches out to help me stand before leaning forward to snag his wallet from the coffee table and retrieve a condom. He throws the foil square on the cushion beside him, then demands, "Come here."

He pulls me down onto his lap, my legs straddling his thighs, his rock-hard member nestled between us, and I bend my head to capture his lips with mine.

He deepens the kiss, and our tongues duel passionately. Why is it that just kissing Drew is far more exciting than sex with a couple of the guys from my past? Of course, I know it's because when Drew kisses me or touches me, I melt into a puddle of longing. Every brush of his lips or touch of his fingers reminds me of how good he feels filling me with his large cock.

Less than an hour ago, I told myself I wasn't going to fall into his arms again, even though that's exactly what I wanted to do. One small slip of my defenses is all it took to be where I am now. Naked and wrapped tightly around him.

He greedily cups my breasts in his palms, gently massaging their fullness, squeezing and then tracing a finger around each pebbled peak. A soft moan slips from my mouth into his.

His lips begin to move away, and I want to chase them. But as he trails them across my chin and down my neck, I'm okay with where this is going too.

I tilt my head sideways, giving him better access to trail feather-soft kisses across my collarbone, ending with a light nip on my shoulder.

"This is what I wanted to do last night," he mumbles against my skin. I loosen my hold around his neck and lean back against his arm holding me.

"You just had to ask," I tell him sweetly as he continues his path down to the swell of my breasts.

He reaches his free hand up to pinch my oversensitive nipple, and a breath catches in my throat. "Did you like that?" he murmurs, lifting his head briefly. I nod vigorously.

"Baby, use your words, or I won't know what things you like

best."

I grab his face between my palms, my eyes locked on his. "Drew, I like you kissing me. I like you licking me. I like you sucking, pinching, tweaking, rubbing me. But most of all, I like you fucking me. Are those enough words for you?"

I can't believe I'm saying these things out loud. These are the thoughts that belong in my head, not shared.

He chuckles. "Plenty. And that's a long list of things you like, so I better get started." And he does, bending his head to the pebbled tip he just pinched to soothe it with his hot breath and then his tongue. He circles my areola, then lavishes soft kisses on it before shifting his attention to my other bared breast.

Oh my God! I'm about to have wild day sex—another first.

I wonder why I don't feel more self-conscious about being completely naked in Drew's arms while he remains fully clothed. In a strange way, it's freeing when the man you're with is appreciating every inch of your body. Even the bits you don't really like, but he doesn't seem to even notice. It's the sexiest damn feeling. I throw my head back and arch my spine, pushing my tits farther forward.

I want him to work his way across every inch of my upper body. My core clenches and my heart races with each touch of his lips and graze of his teeth. The occasional love bites add to the flames of desire building in me. I want him to feel this desperate too. I want to sink down onto his cock and make him scream my name.

"Drew, I need you filling me up," I whisper softly.

He lifts his head and pulls me in closer. "We need a condom." He picks up the one on the cushion beside us and makes quick work of opening it and sheathing himself.

I help him to slide his gray sweats farther down to his ankles, then coming back up, straddle his thighs again, and ask, "How do we do this without hurting you?"

A fire flares in the depths of his slate-gray eyes, and that's all the warning I get.

NINE

Drew

Grabbing firmly to her hips, I throw her down beside me on the sofa cushions. "Let me be clear, sexy lady. I am more than capable of pleasuring you without hurting myself. I'm not completely helpless." My words are abruptly delivered with an edge of ice. I know Katie didn't mean to imply anything with her words, but they hit a raw nerve.

She's splayed out before me, naked, her eyes wide, her lips slightly parted, and all I want is to be inside her. But before she can reply, I lift and spread her legs. Holding them up and open, I bury my face in her glistening folds. I'm not gentle as I lick, suck, and devour her pussy.

Her increasingly loud moans feed my frenzy. The way she's gripping my head tightly in both of her hands tells me everything I need to know. She wants this as badly as I do.

I don't let up, and as the sounds coming from her lips reach a crescendo, I plunge two fingers into her channel, curling them up so they hit that spot she liked last time. And like last time, it tips her over the edge.

Her head thrashes from side to side.

Her voice cracks on a groan of release.

Her nails dig into my scalp.

Nothing is held back. She gives me everything. Each drop of passion coats my tongue, and I lap her up.

How could I have forgotten how glorious she is when she comes?

How willingly she exposes herself to me, with a total lack of inhibition that brings me to my knees.

When she finally quiets, her grasp on me easing, I lift my head. Her eyelids flutter open. Her pupils are huge, almost indistinguishable from the darkened brown irises.

Placing my hands under each of her arms, I slide her up the sofa, then impatiently drag my T-shirt over my head and tug my sweatpants off completely. All under her watchful gaze.

Finally, as naked as she is, I climb up her body, positioning myself between her legs, using my good arm to hold as much of my weight off her as possible. I might struggle to walk, but like this, lying on top of her, my injury is negligible.

"Now we can fuck." It's half question, half statement, and when she smiles angelically up at me and opens her legs wider, I sink slowly into her heat. Inch by inch, her walls stretch around me, tight and wet. Katie feels fucking amazing.

Burying my face in her neck, I growl her name in pleasure.

Katie tilts her hips, and I sink deeper into heaven. Rocking gently is all I'm capable of doing without losing my load.

"Don't move until I tell you to," I demand on a raspy breath. She stills, and I mumble, "Good girl," before trailing kisses up her neck and to her sweet lips.

Our kisses are soft, a mere brushing of our lips together, but that doesn't last long. Soon I'm sucking her bottom lip, and she's nipping at mine, our kisses more demanding. I begin to move my hips in a slow pistoning motion. I want this feeling to last, but maybe I'm not going to. Or, judging by the way Katie's nails are now digging into my shoulders, maybe she won't be able to.

I draw my hips back slightly, then thrust them forward again, driving hard into her body. Her "Ahh" as I hit balls deep encourages me to do it again. I want to hear her low moan of pleasure on repeat. I pump into her three more times, and each time, her walls tighten around my dick, squeezing me, taking me closer to release.

I brace my upper body on one arm, glad this is one area of my body that isn't diminished. Then, with my other hand, I tug on her nipple. I know how sensitive her tits are to my touch, and I'm willing to exploit this knowledge. My rhythm increases, our bodies coming together forcefully, more frenzied and out of control.

Her gasping breaths intermingle with desperate cries for more. I give her more, yet still she begs. I want to give her everything.

Another plunge into her.

A punishing pinch of her nipple.

And my balls draw up. I can't hold back anymore. But I don't have to, as her knees grip my waist tightly and she screams out my name with her orgasm.

I'm coming long and hard too, thick streams shooting from my body into the condom. Our release as one. My vision blurs. Nothing else exists but this woman in this exquisite moment.

Drained and exhausted, I collapse on top of her with an "Oomph." My arms shake, weak, sapped of all strength and no longer able to support my upper body.

"Wow! You are kind of heavy," comes Katie's muffled voice from under me.

"Shit." I separate from her, then roll to the side. "Sorry, I didn't mean to squash you."

She giggles. It's a light tinkling sound that makes me want to say something clever so she'll do it again. But all I've got is, "Are you okay?"

"Perfect," she replies a little drowsily as she turns on her side and throws an arm and leg over my body. I like this, even if our movements are restricted by the small sofa. I've never been a big fan of snuggling with a woman after we've fucked, but I really do like having Katie sprawled over me. The strength in my arms has returned, and I pull her in closer.

Comfortably entwined, I feel like we should talk about what just happened. How did a contract discussion turn into steamy hot sex?

"Katie?"

"Hmm?" she murmurs into my chest.

"Do you want to talk about what just happened? Because I think our business relationship just got a lot more complicated." My head is beginning to clear, and it's important I know where we stand here. We probably should have had this chat before we decided to fuck each other's brains out. But it's too late for that now.

Katie leans up and away from me slightly. Distractingly, her beautiful tits are visible, and I want to run my tongue over her nipples again. She draws a deep breath in and they brush against my upper body.

"Drew, look at me. What just happened was two consenting adults coming together in a moment of passion. This has nothing to do with business and everything to do with pleasure. I have no trouble drawing a hard line between business and pleasure. Do you?" Katie's little speech is delivered in what I expect is her boss lady voice. It's firm and clear, with a heavy coating of *don't mess with me*. It's hard to believe this is the same woman who, minutes ago, came apart in my arms, not once but twice.

I let her words sink in before replying. "I've no trouble at all understanding the difference between business and what we just did, which was pure pleasure. I'm glad we're clear. But I do have one question; can we do this again?" I point a finger back and forth between us.

She smiles, and it lights up her face. "Of course."

"Great. How about a shower first?"

I ease away from her and up to sitting. I quickly deal with the condom, then contemplate how I'm going to get to the shower without the crutches. The thought of Katie seeing my scarred, naked body hobbling to the shower on crutches is a hit to the ego I don't think I want to take.

Katie sits up beside me, flings her legs over the edge of the sofa, and stands up before me.

"Would you like to lean on me to get to the shower?" It's like she heard the conversation rolling around in my head. I take her offered hands and stand. Then, throwing one arm across her shoulders like we did before, we slowly make our way into my bedroom and the adjoining bathroom.

The shower in the cottage has been perfect with my injury. It's a large tiled space running across one end of the bathroom, the only divider a glass panel that runs to halfway. With a solid wooden stool placed under the rainfall shower head, it's been a safe way for me to shower alone or, as is the case now, with a friend.

Water pours over our bodies. Me sitting on the stool, Katie standing between my legs.

She reaches for my bottle of shampoo, holds it out to me, and asks, "Will you wash my hair?"

I take the offered bottle and smile. "I've never washed a

woman's hair before, so there are no guarantees that it won't end up a tangled mess."

She laughs. "I'm willing to take the risk."

She sits on the tiled floor between my legs, her back to me. I pour some of the shampoo into my palms and begin to lather the foamy liquid through those beautiful dark strands. It's surprisingly erotic, massaging my fingers into her scalp while she sits before me, her head resting between my thighs and only inches from my hardening cock. I'm mesmerized by the way the same rivulets of warm water running down my body flow over hers.

Even when the water runs clear, I continue, moving from her head down her neck and shoulders and then farther still, over her breasts, cupping her slippery tits in my palms and massaging their fullness.

I'm so hard for her again.

TEN

Drew

A little while later, we're back in the kitchen, clean, dressed, and hungry.

I lean against the open fridge door, staring at the contents. "I'd like to offer you something to eat, but all I have are the basics. Some tins of soup, ham, cheese, bread, eggs, and milk are the lot until my regular order of groceries gets delivered tomorrow." I straighten and look over to where she's standing at the end of the countertop a few feet away. She's doing up the last of the buttons on her shirt and hiding that little white lacy bra from my sight. Her sexy underwear is something else.

"How about ham and cheese toasties?" she asks, smiling like she knows I was just checking her out.

"Great idea."

We work together preparing the simple meal and when the toasties are ready, Katie carries them on a tray out to the deck. She's so easy to be with. Oddly, with her, it doesn't annoy me when she asks if I'm okay, and it no longer feels uncomfortable having her help me. When she insisted on washing me in the shower while I sat on the stool, it was anything but uncomfortable. Her soapy, soft hands running freely over every inch of my body was soothing. It even felt good when she sat on the tiles and took my right leg into her lap to gently wash the scarred flesh.

I'm noticing that she doesn't look at me like I'm helpless. Not like my family. I love my family dearly, but back in London, they were getting on my last nerve. Constantly asking if I was okay. My mother's eyes filling with tears whenever she looked at my shattered legs. I don't need other people reminding me that my body is broken. It's fucking obvious every time I move.

It's a tough pill to swallow, that my body can no longer be relied on to perform the simplest of tasks. It's been a long time since I've felt so out of my depth. I was trained by the best in the SAS to be the best. I can survive extreme conditions with little more than the skills my training gave me. I can protect myself physically with or without a weapon in my hands. But that was all before the accident, and I'm struggling to come to terms with my new reality. Vulnerability is not something I've ever been familiar with. I'm worried this might be an emotion I'll have to learn to live with.

Over our late lunch, we've talked about where we grew up and our families back home—mine in Scotland and hers in the States. And now we've just finished talking a little more about my injuries, the surgeries, and my recovery. The conversation flows freely from one topic to the next.

It was nice to be able to speak calmly and openly about my recovery with Katie, even if we didn't cover my biggest concern.

I'm not ready to talk to anyone about the possibility that I may be left permanently injured. I fear saying those words out loud will turn the maybe into reality, and I'm determined to be optimistic. Even if the doctor's prognosis is that I'll be left with a significant limp because my right leg is now a little shorter than my left. How noticeable the limp will be is all down to me.

I finish eating and place my plate back on the table. Over the last few minutes, we've fallen into a comfortable silence, each of us gazing out at the ocean, caught up in our own thoughts.

Katie places her plate on top of mine, and it looks like she might be ready to go. I don't want her to leave yet; I'm enjoying her company.

"Will you tell me more about your family?" I ask. I want to learn more about her, and she's an amusing storyteller.

She turns to look at me. "What would you like to know?"

"I don't know. Maybe something that I can't find by Googling the Carlson family."

"Ah, the secrets and skeletons in the family closet. I don't know that I can trust you with those."

"The British government trusted me with secrets, so you can too." I hold up my hand and promise. "I swear I won't sell the Carlson family secrets to the tabloids, pass them on to the intelligence agencies, or sell them on the dark web."

She laughs. "Honestly, there aren't even any secrets to tell. Although I guess my early years haven't made it to the internet. My mom and stepdad did a pretty good job of keeping us kids out of the spotlight until we turned eighteen."

"All right, then tell me more about your early years."

"Well, my biological dad died in a car accident when I was a baby. I never really knew him. All I know is what Mom told me, which was that he was really excited to be a dad. I don't remember much about our life before the Carlsons, because I was seven when Mom married my stepdad. But I do have some memories of Mom being sad a lot. I remember walking into her room at night when I couldn't sleep, and she would be crying. It's not a clear memory, and I'm not sure how often it happened." She shakes her head, and still damp strands of dark hair dance across her shoulders before she continues. "I've never told anyone that. I haven't even spoken to Mom about it. Anyway, everything changed when she met my stepdad. She smiled and laughed, and really, I don't think she's stopped since. We moved in with the Carlsons when they married, and my stepdad adopted me. He wanted me to be his daughter in every way possible. To me, he's just Dad, the only father I've known."

"Thank you for sharing that," I tell her before leaning across the small table and placing a gentle kiss on her lips. This isn't like the frenzied, desperate kisses from earlier. This kiss is sweet, matching our leisurely mood.

"Now it's your turn," Katie says.

"There's not much to tell. My alcoholic father was a mean drunk. My mother worked too hard trying to compensate and provide for her five children. It was a relief to all of us when he died from too much booze. The only good thing about my childhood was my best friend, Aaron. He saved my life more times than I can count." I stop to take a breath before saying, "I'm sorry, it's not a nice story like yours." She reaches to hold my hand, which is resting on the table, her dark eyes filled with compassion.

I feel the usual shutter come down over my emotions. I don't need anyone to feel sorry for me.

Katie pulls her hand back sharply. "I should really be going. I've got some work to do back at the bed-and-breakfast," she says before standing, picking up our dirty plates, and racing back through the door with them.

Way to go, arsehole. Way to ruin an afternoon, I admonish myself as I stand to see her out. But before I'm even through the door, she already has her bag on her shoulder and is ready to leave.

She glances my way briefly. "I'll see you tomorrow morning about the contract. Have a good evening." Then she's walking toward the front door.

I mumble a goodbye, and she's gone, the door closing with a thud behind her.

A stab of disappointment hits me.

ELEVEN

Katie

I thought leaving Drew yesterday to return to the bed-and-breakfast with the excuse of having to catch up on work emails would allow me to sort through the churning emotions that are filling the pit of my stomach.

Our first night together after the awards party was fantastic, memorable, and special in the context of a one-night stand. Just one night to look back on fondly, remember over cocktails with friends and maybe even use as inspiration for late-night sessions with my wand. All the things I did in the two months since.

It wasn't supposed to happen again. But I guess from the moment I learned Drew was the reclusive A. V. Campbell, I suspected, almost subconsciously hoped, it would happen again. And now that it has,

I'm not sure how I feel about it.

The man is way too good at all things sex related and could be dangerous to my heart. Already, he has me wanting to stay longer than I planned. But I won't.

I was only ever going to stay till the contract was signed, and, based on the email from Drew late last night stating he was ready to sign, that will happen this morning.

Once that signed contract is in my hand, there won't be any reason for me to stay. I can jump straight in my car and be back in my Kensington terrace house by late afternoon. Tomorrow, back in the office, I can hand Drew's account over to my very capable chief editor, and I can then go back to treating my time with Drew as just one more steamy escapade. It's clear to me that's how he sees our time together—casual and fun.

There was a moment on the deck yesterday afternoon when I thought it could have been more, but then, when I got too close to learning more about the complex man underneath the perfect façade, I was instantly shut down.

I take another leisurely bite of my freshly baked blueberry muffin and wash it down with a sip of English breakfast tea. Replacing the floral fine bone china cup on the matching saucer, I look out the window at what is going to be another beautiful late spring day. The weather in Cornwall is certainly nicer than the all too frequent gray London days.

It's only been a couple of days, but I'm going to miss Cornwall, especially these breakfasts served by Mary, the middle-aged owner of the residence. Her blueberry muffins are to die for, and she can even make a cup of tea taste okay. To say I wasn't a fan of the nation's traditional drink when I first arrived would be an understatement. But, like everything British, it has slowly grown on me.

Mary bustles back into the quaint, sunny breakfast room. "Would you like another cuppa? Or muffin?" She really is adorable, with her cheery good mornings, excellent baking skills, and flamboyant flowery apron collection. Every day, she's worn a different version, and today's bright yellow sunflower one might be my favorite.

"Mary, I swear you spoil me. But I can't eat or drink another thing, and I really do need to be going." She places a paper bag with two muffins inside on the table for me to take to Drew. The same as she did yesterday.

She begins clearing the empty plates from the table. "It's been such a pleasure having you stay with us. I'm going to miss you, pet." I smile again at her use of the endearment *pet*. It's such a funny way to affectionately refer to someone.

I stand, and she pulls me in for a warm, motherly hug. She has six adult children and five grandchildren, so she has perfected the motherly hug. It makes me a little homesick for my own mom, my dad, and my brothers. We're a close family of huggers, and I miss seeing them in person, even though I speak to them most days.

"Mary, thank you so much for making me feel so comfortable and welcome."

"Any friend of Drew's is a friend of ours. And you will come back to see us and Drew again, won't you, pet?" It turns out that Mary and her husband own the cottage that Drew is renting. It really is a small village.

I smile. "I'd like to come back to see you, but I'm not sure I can." She reaches out for another hug, and when I say goodbye, her smile is not as bright. It's the truth. I would like to come back to see her, but as far as Drew wanting me to come down again now that the contract is signed? I doubt it.

I collect my bag from the hallway and leave with a final wave to Mary and her husband, who has come to stand beside her with his hand resting gently on her shoulder. She told me they've been married fifty-two years. Now there are some relationship goals.

Dropping my overnight bag onto the back seat, I place my tote, phone, and Drew's bag of muffins on the passenger seat and drive one last time to Drew's place.

My mind turns to the man I'm going to see in a few minutes, perhaps for the last time in a long while. The thought makes me sad. I feel like I've learned so much more about Drew. He's no longer the one-night stand who was great in bed, although he's certainly the best sexual partner I've ever had. It turns out Drew is totally different from what I imagined when I first met him months ago on the dance floor. In fact, that first impression of him being a pretty boy player couldn't have been further from the truth. There is so much more to him. A depth and sensitivity that I guess he really only reveals in his writing, and it scares me a little that the more I learn, the more I want to know. I guess I could pretend that I want to understand what makes him tick purely from a business point of view, but that would be lying to both him and me.

***

Ten minutes later, I'm pulling into the gravel lay-by beside Drew's cottage. Things were a little awkward between us when I left yesterday, but I'm determined to brush that aside and pretend everything is fine.

I grab my things from the passenger seat and wander to his door. I knock lightly, then turn the knob because Drew is adamant that I walk straight in. He is sitting at the desk in the corner of the room, his laptop open in front of him, and with my interruption, he spins in the chair to face me.

He removes a pair of glasses and smiles tentatively at me. "Good morning," he says.

Damn, the man and his ability to look hot even when he's reading. "Hey. I seem to always be catching you in the middle of something. Yesterday, you were half naked on a table, being massaged by a large muscled man, and today you're working and wearing a sexy pair of glasses."

He chokes out a laugh and looks down at the glasses in his hand. "What a crack, you think my glasses are sexy?" He then puts them back on and holds his hands wide in front of him. "Come here and have at it, then."

He seems to be taking the same approach as me and ignoring my speedy, uncomfortable departure yesterday.

"Oh, please. I said the glasses are sexy …"

He holds a hand to his heart. "You wound me now." I roll my eyes but still can't keep the smile from my face.

"I'm not here to stroke your ego, Mr. Campbell." His eyebrows shoot up, and I realize that what I've said could be taken in a completely different way, and, of course, it is.

"You can stroke all you want, baby. Especially when you call me Mr. Campbell." He waggles his eyebrows suggestively, and a blush suffuses my cheeks, much to my dismay.

I'm very tempted to take him up on the offer. His hair is tousled and damp, no doubt from a recent shower. His white T-shirt is stretched tightly over the lean body I got to run my hands over yesterday. Thankfully, he has jeans on and not sweats, though the way the faded denim stretches over his thighs is almost as good. I notice everything about Drew as he sits at his desk, looking at me.

When he's in this lighthearted mood, I want to pick up where we left off yesterday, but I can't. Not today. I'm here to get the contract signed. No distractions. Especially not the kind we engaged in yesterday.

"Mr. Campbell," I say in my most professional manner, "I'm here to talk business today, so can you keep your mind out of the bedroom?"

"Aye, the boss lady is in the house." He holds up a bundle of papers in his hand. "One signed contract right here. And thank you for including the section around maintaining my privacy."

My head tilts to the side. This is something I've wondered

about from the moment I started dealing with A. V. Campbell. I couldn't understand why there were no pictures of Drew anywhere. He explained yesterday that no one outside his circle of friends and family knows that he's the world-famous author. But he never elaborated on why.

"Why the need for the privacy? If you don't mind me asking."

"I don't mind you asking. It's no big mystery. I'm just a private person, and I want to live my life quietly, out of the public spotlight. I'll do the book signings mentioned in the contract. I'm not stupid. I realize the importance of promotion. I'd just like it to be kept to a minimum." He looks down at the floor for a moment, then continues. "It's also a bit of a protective mechanism because, like most authors, I worry that my next book will be a flop."

"Really? I never would have thought you'd suffer insecurities. You're a brilliant writer." His first book was well deserving of the accolades it won.

"I'm human, Katie."

I nod. The arrogance I saw in him that first night is all a façade, and you don't have to dig too deep to see the authentic man beneath. When he's willing to let you get close enough to dig.

Grinning broadly, I walk over to take the papers from him. "Thank you. And I'll swap you two of Mary's blueberry muffins." Taking the bag of muffins with one hand, he snags my wrist with the other and pulls me toward him.

It catches me by surprise, and before I escape his hold, he has me on his lap, one arm around me, and the other reaching up to touch my lips. "I'll never be able to see pink lipstick again without thinking of how good it looked smeared on my cock yesterday."

"Rose," I mumble as his thumb traces along my bottom lip.

"What?"

"It's rose, not pink," I murmur, not even sure why I'm talking lipstick when all I want is his lips on mine, not his thumb.

A deep, throaty laugh bursts from him. "Don't care what color it is, baby. I just want it marking me." My eyes pop open wide. How did we get here? My teeth worry my bottom lip. This wasn't my plan today.

His face grows serious. "I'm sorry about yesterday. I'm not used to sharing about my personal life."

"I get it. You're a private person," I reply with a smile.

"Exactly." He laughs at me throwing his words back at him, then begins to rub his thumb lightly over my lips. "Stay another day. Here with me. The contract is all done, so you have what you came for." I'm struggling to resist the temptation of his touch. All my fuzzy mind can process in this moment is that I want more. But just like yesterday, I don't know what he's offering, so I hold back.

"I can't. I have to be back in London tomorrow morning," I tell him, and it's the truth. I have the weekly executive meeting to attend virtually.

"But you could stay a few more hours," he suggests.

"Maybe" slips from my mouth before I even think to stop it. It's like he's cast a spell over me, and I no longer have the strength to deny him whatever he wants.

"Good girl," he responds gruffly before entwining his fingers in my hair and bringing our lips together.

I sink into his kisses and the heat of his body. The heady scent of his spicy cologne adds another tempting element to being up close and personal with Drew. His hand gently tilts my head, giving him better access to my lips. My bones turn to jelly as his hands run all over my body. He groans into my shoulder.

I don't speak; just act, undoing the top five buttons on my favorite electric-blue silk shirt. Each strip of skin bared is an invitation for Drew to trail kisses lower. I roughly tug the shirt from the waistband of my black pants, and as it snags, I pull harder, not caring if the delicate fabric rips. Finally managing to get the offending shirt off,

I work on removing his.

When it's over his head, I smash my lips back to his. It's a hot, wet kiss, and when his tongue slips between my parted lips, my body quivers with need.

He pulls me back from him, and I grumble my complaint.

"I need you naked," he tells me, and when I'm too slow to move, he pleads, "Now, baby."

I stand up, kick off my heels, and remove my pants until I'm left standing in today's blue lace lingerie. He smiles as his eyes trail up, then down, leaving my skin heated and flushed everywhere his gaze touches.

"Everything," he demands, waggling his finger at me. I slowly remove my bra and then panties. A grin stretches wider on my mouth as his breathing becomes more labored when my breasts and then pussy are revealed to him.

Somewhere during this, he unbuckled his belt and unzipped his jeans, and now his cock is fisted in his hand. With his free arm, he drags me to straddle his hips.

But then he stops abruptly. "Fuck," he curses, then drops his head to mine. "We can't."

"What?" I gasp. The one-hundred-and-eighty-degree change is making my head spin.

"We can't. I just realized I don't have any more condoms." His voice is croaky, like it pains him to say the words.

I lean back, then take his face between my palms. "We don't have to use one. I'm on the pill, and you're the only person I've had sex with over the last year. I'm clean."

He stares at me, then realizing I'm waiting for him to say something, he says quickly in his deep, throaty bedroom voice, "Same for me … What I mean is I'm clean, and obviously, you were my last too." He mirrors my action and places his hands on my cheeks. "Are you sure?"

I nod but also say, "Yes, absolutely." I don't want to be accused again of not using my words.

"Ride me," he growls. I lift up, then position his head at my entrance and sink slowly down onto him. The stretch as he fills me is exquisite. When I'm fully seated, I ride him *hard*. All thoughts of leaving are replaced by a need to cling like a limpet to Drew's body. Our panting fills the air in the cottage as we race each other to completion.

Desperately.

Hungrily.

Taking every drop of passion from each other's body until we're shouting our releases, his cock pulsing inside me as he fills me with cum.

Collapsing, sweaty and exhausted, our limbs still entwined, I try to catch my breath.

Drew lifts his head from my shoulder and looks me in the eye. "You … are … pure … dead … brilliant."

I squint at him. "Sorry, but I have no idea what that means. Do you think I'm clever?"

"Pretty much. Brilliant, amazing, beautiful, wicked." He peppers kisses across my face with each word, moving to my shoulders and the tops of my breasts. The kisses are soft, like a delicate feather brushing over my sensitive buds. I can't hold back a girlish giggle. I've never been much of a giggler, but Drew seems to have the ability to elicit them from me in bubbly bursts.

I pull his head up and drag his lips back to mine. I can't get enough of his kisses, especially after that mind-blowing orgasm.

I'm falling for him, exactly what I didn't want to happen.

TWELVE

Drew

Like every time since that first night together, Katie is insatiable. The feel of her dripping folds encasing my bare cock is fucking amazing. It's been nearly ten years since I had the pleasure of being with a woman without a condom.

She wiggles a little, my cock still buried deep inside her. "I forgot how messy this can be," she exclaims.

I laugh as I reach down beside the chair to retrieve my discarded T-shirt. "Here, use this to clean up until we can get you in the shower."

We make it to the shower and when the water is cascading over our bodies, she straddles me again while I sit on the stool. I suspect every shower from now on will be spent reliving this moment. The sex is less frenzied as she sinks slowly down onto my still erect cock, then instead of riding me hard and fast, rises and falls in a slow steady rhythm that is just as spectacular. Our bodies completely in sync. I love it.

Quickly, I pull myself up on that random thought. What am I thinking? This is just meant to be a bit of fun for both of us. There are no serious feelings involved here. There can't be.

Katie lifts her head, looking me straight in the eye. "What's wrong? You suddenly pulled away."

Shit! I didn't even realize I had. "Nothing. Just a twinge in my leg."

"Oh my God," she exclaims, crawling off my hips and removing me from her heat. "I'm so sorry. I didn't mean to hurt you. I forgot all about being careful." She looks so cute with the flush on her cheeks and her fingers tugging at her bottom lip. Guilt hits me like a punch. She wasn't hurting me at all. It was just a stupid, readily available excuse.

I reach up and tuck a stray lock of dark, wet hair behind her ear. "Katie, you didn't hurt me. Really, it was just a muscle twinge. It happens all the time." At least these words are true. "But since you're up, I guess we better get out. You need to be going if you don't want to be driving back to London in the dark."

She frowns at the reminder. I would have liked her to stay the night, but I guess it's for the best she goes. Sex with Katie is intense, mind-blowing, and should be taken in small doses, or feelings may develop. Something neither of us wants.

We dry off, then walk naked into the bedroom to change. Ignoring my own clothes, I watch, mesmerized, as Katie bends to step one foot, then the next, into her lace panties. I shouldn't enjoy seeing her put clothes on, but when her bare butt is right there in front of me, it's very tempting to grab a hold of her hips and bury my cock deep inside her again.

I clear my throat. She straightens before glancing over her shoulder. A cheeky smile tips up her lips. She knows I was checking her out.

I give her a wink, then start to dress too. "I guess it's back to us emailing again when you return to London."

It's the first time any mention has been made of what comes next. It's like I've just dropped a bombshell; the silence is deafening.

She turns to face me, her brows wrinkled in a frown. "I think we've moved beyond just emailing. Don't you?" I watch as she slips the straps of her bra on and reaches around to her back to do it up. The action pushes her breasts forward, and I want to fondle them again, but my chance to do that has passed.

I shrug. "Aye, we do have a sexual chemistry that could blow up a laboratory if someone tried to bottle it." This is my attempt at lightening the mood, but it's fallen flat, given the death stare Katie is directing my way.

Honestly, I've no idea what she wants from me. I'm still barely able to walk and driving is still weeks away, so going to London is out of the question. Besides, I have a book to write and a deadline to meet if I don't want to be in breach of the contract I only just signed.

I watch her slip her arms into the sleeves of her silk shirt, not knowing how to put what I'm feeling into words. It's stupid really, that I can't find the right words when I need them the most.

Finally, I split the silence. "I guess what I'm trying to say is that it's best if we go back to business. I've got this book to write, and you have a publishing empire to run." She finishes tucking her shirt into her black trousers, then, putting one hand on her hip, she stares at me.

It's awkward standing before her in only my boxer shorts. This could have waited until we were both dressed.

"Well, that's clear then. You fucked me, and now we're done.

This is my cue to leave." She brushes past me on her way out of the room. Shit, she must be angry to be swearing. I've no idea what I just said that caused her to explode like that. I'm just trying to be realistic.

"Katie …"

"What?" she asks sternly, stopping at the doorway.

"I was trying to say that it's best we don't make any promises. Now is not the right time for us. I need to focus on healing physically and getting this book finished. I can't let distractions get in my way."

Her laser focus is nailing me to the spot. "Great. So I'm just a distraction. Wow, that's harsh … but good to know before we go any further here. Drew, I didn't ask for promises. I just expect a little respect rather than feeling like … I'm being kicked out now that you got what you wanted." I reach for her hand, but she spins out of my reach and leaves me staring after her departing figure. I guess I fucked that up.

It takes me about ten minutes to dress in sweats and a T-shirt, the frustration at not being able to do it quicker turning my mood even more sour. She's gone, and I literally can't fucking stop her.

I grab my crutches beside the bed and hobble out of my bedroom. My shoulder bumps hard into the wall when I find Katie sitting stiffly on a stool at the kitchen counter. She has one shapely leg crossed on top of the other, and her foot swings in the air, a lethal looking black heel hanging from it, ready to inflict damage. From the way she's staring at me, that could be what she is planning.

I thought she had gone back to London without saying goodbye. Relief has me slumping over the crutches as I lean on them heavily.

"Katie, I'm sorry. What I wanted to say came out all wrong."

"I don't need this crap," she says harshly.

"Neither do I." I move to stand before her, toe to toe. Her sweet perfume is still faintly swirling around her after the shower, and like a siren song, it draws me in closer to her.

"I was trying to say—"

She raises her hand to stop me. "I know what you were trying to say. This thing between us was just a moment in time, and now we need to return to real life. You need to get stronger and finish a book. And as you put it, I need to return to London to run a business."

"I'm sorry it can't be more." It feels like a lame response, because I do wish we could meet up again.

"Me too," she whispers. She stands, lightly kisses me on the cheek, and with a "Goodbye, Drew," she collects her bag and really does leave this time. I lean against the kitchen counter, and a few minutes later, I hear her car start up and crunch across the gravel driveway as she reverses, then drives away.

Back to London.

Back to her life there.

And out of mine.

THIRTEEN

Katie

Present Day

I slam my cell back on the desk, and luckily, the stack of papers strewn across it cushions the impact. It's nine on a Monday morning, and any good vibes I managed to return home with after the weekend in Bath with Sarah have already disappeared. My eyes trail across my messy desk to where my cell bounced to. This isn't the first time I've mistreated my phone following a conversation with my annoyingly overbearing oldest brother, Hunter.

I feel like I'm constantly having to prove myself, and it's not fair. I'm pretty sure he doesn't treat Logan the same, and he's only a few months older than me. I brush my hair back from my face, gathering it in my hand before tying it back into a messy bun with the hairband I always have handy on my wrist. This simple task gives me a moment to breathe and regroup, then let the tension go. A little relaxation technique I learned a few years ago.

I love my brothers dearly, and honestly, I couldn't exist without them. But as is usually the case with big brothers, they each have their moments of driving me crazy. Today it's Hunter's turn. I'm not sure what's worse: when he's here checking over my shoulder, or when he constantly tells me what to do from back in the states, like a puppeteer pulling the strings.

I've been running the London office successfully for nearly a year now, and I wish he could understand that I don't need him to come to my rescue each time some decision is needed. I'm the one best placed to know what's right for the British market and my team. I have a master's degree in business from Harvard and six years of experience in publishing. I'm well qualified to do this job.

I allow myself one final growl of frustration, then open up a new email to Hunter on my laptop and begin typing, explaining clearly and factually why I want us to hold off for another six months on the planned expansion into the European market.

About five minutes later, certainly no more than ten, his reply hits my inbox. He agrees. A smile breaks out across my face when I read his response. There is no explanation, just that he agrees. It's very unlike him. In fact, for the last couple of weeks, he hasn't been acting like his usual self. Oh well. I'll be home soon for Christmas, and I can find out what's going on from Blake and Logan.

I tap my pen on the desk. Actually, my brothers are probably clueless. I'll ask Blake's new girlfriend, Bec. She and I have become friendly since they became an item officially a few months ago.

A few minutes later, another new email grabs my attention. It's the heading, *Author A. V. Campbell Proposed Book Signing UK Tour*

Dates, that stands out, not the fact that it was sent by my marketing and promotions manager, Jackie. My stomach clenches into a solid pit of dread. There is no more avoiding the inevitable. Drew's book is done, and he'll be coming into the London office to finalize details for the book signing tour. Soon, not today or tomorrow, but soon, I'm going to have to read Drew's book and probably meet with him too. It's part of my job.

For the rest of the day, every time I go to my inbox, I think about Drew's edited manuscript sitting as an attachment on the book tour email. I've never been a clock watcher, but today I am, and by four in the afternoon, I can't take it anymore. I pack up my desk for the day and leave.

Going home to my empty townhouse doesn't feel much better. I drop my keys on the hall table, hang my Armani wool coat on the hallstand, and kick off my heels, leaving them right there. I can't be bothered to bend and pick them up today. I plod along the thickly carpeted hallway to the stairs that lead down to the kitchen on the lower ground level. Today, even the soft cream wool underfoot after a day in heels doesn't help me brush off the workday stresses.

Downstairs in the kitchen, I pour myself a glass of red wine and take it through to my home office, which leads out to a small courtyard. I don't go out. The sun has already set, and being December, it's chilly without a coat. During the spring and summer, the ten-foot square space is a great little sun trap. The garden running along one end is filled to overflowing with scented climbing roses and flowering annuals in pinks and purples. It's a little oasis.

I flop down into the comfy chair in the corner of my warm, cozy office and take a sip of wine. Pulling my phone from my pocket, I call Sarah. I need my friend to cheer me up. She is about the only one who can talk me down from the anxiety I'm feeling at having to see Drew again.

She answers after one ring. "Hey, hun. What's happening?"

"Hi, I just needed to talk. I'm freaking out a little."

I hear her loud sigh through the phone. "Let me guess. Drew?" It's not hard for her to guess when she knows the whole sorry saga.

"Of course it is. When else do I freak out? Actually, don't answer that."

Sarah has been on the receiving end of a few of my emergency freak-out calls. And it's fair to say most of the recent ones have been Drew related, but sometimes they relate to my brothers.

"Come on, then. Hit me with the latest."

"Drew's book signing tour dates are being finalized," I draw in a deep breath, then, as if I've just finished a marathon, I pant out, "which means he'll be in the office next week … And I'll have to see him again."

"Whoa! You sound like you're losing your shit."

"Maybe because I … am … losing … my … shit. And the shit is about to get real." I've known this was coming, just not so soon.

Jackie spoke to me a couple of months ago about scheduling the book tour for the end of January because these things need to be planned way in advance. The author then comes into the office for a final confirmation six weeks before. Next week will be seven weeks to the start of Drew's book tour, but with Christmas in between, Jackie has decided to bring the meeting forward.

"Girl, please calm down. Why do you have to see him when he comes into the office?"

"Do I need to remind you that I'm the boss? It's my job." I rub my eyes with the stress of it all.

"Exactly, you're the boss. You were planning to go to the States at the end of next week for the Christmas break. Surely, you could leave a little earlier. Maybe work out of the Manhattan office for the week or something?"

My friend is a genius. "Oh my God, you're the best. It's perfect. You're right. I can leave early, then I won't have to see him until

January. If I'm lucky, maybe not even then." With Jackie handling all the details, my involvement should be minimal. If I have to, I can call into the meeting next week from the States. At least I won't have to see him face-to-face. My mind races with thoughts of bringing my travel plans forward.

I tune back into Sarah's voice, and she says, "Do I need to remind you of our conversation from the weekend? You are supposed to be moving on. Remember, drinks with the neighbor."

I take another sip of wine. "Well, I can't ask him now. I'll be flying to the States next weekend. Perhaps after New Year's I can move on."

Her light chuckle can be heard over the line. "Sure. Any excuse."

She's right. It's another excuse so I can cling to the possibility that when I see Drew next, our timing might be right.

Sarah's voice comes through my earbuds again. "Look, I get that things are going to be awkward with Drew after your tumble in the sheets down in Cornwall, but that was months ago. Why are you so worried about seeing him again?"

Sarah doesn't really get being hung up on a guy. She's never had that problem. Men are always hung up on her, while she remains happily carefree. Her heart never takes a beating. I'm the complete opposite. I tend to fall quickly. I'm honest enough with myself to know I was falling for Drew. Probably from that first night, but definitely after the time we spent together in Cornwall.

"Hey, are you still there?" Sarah asks when I sit silently, looking down at my phone.

"Yes, still here … Honest answer? I don't trust myself around him. It's like he casts a spell over me, and before I know it, I'm stripping off my clothes and jumping his bones. Even when I tell myself I'm not going to."

"Is he that good?"

"Unfortunately, he is."

***

Three days later, there's a knock on my door, and when it opens, Laura, my personal assistant, steps into my office. I raise my head, and the worried expression on her face has me bracing for bad news or details of some new crisis. A print run to be redone, a deadline missed.

But the reality is even more shocking when she tells me, "Andrew Campbell is in reception, and he's asking to see you."

My mouth drops open, and literally nothing comes out in the form of words. Just a pathetic, weak excuse for a gasp. So many questions spin through my head.

Why is he here?

Why has he asked to see me?

I try to pull myself together by shuffling, then straightening the papers on my desk. I don't want to lose it in front of Laura.

When every piece of paper is neatly stacked, I continue to stare down at my shaking hand and say quietly, "Please ask Mr. Campbell to wait for me in the conference room. Thank you, Laura."

Laura leaves my office, and as the door clicks closed again, I release the breath I was holding. Damn that man. There's no avoiding Drew anymore. I'll have to see him. But not in my office. Not anywhere private. The conference room with its wall of glass is the complete opposite.

I take a few more deep breaths before standing and walking to the door. It's only a short walk along the corridor to the room but each step feels like I'm dragging a heavy load. I stop briefly outside the open door to calm my breathing and slip what I hope is a neutral mask over my features. One step into the room is all it takes for his familiar cologne to reach me and pull me back in time. It beckons me closer, but I resist the temptation. He doesn't turn, but he knows I'm here. His back straightens imperceptibly, and it's hard to ignore the way his shirt stretches across his broad shoulders. My fingertips tingle at the memory of how his muscles felt under my hands.

When I draw level with his chair, I say, "Drew," and it catches on a breath. Not firm and professional like I wanted, but fluttery and weak.

He stands—unaided, I notice—before he steps toward me. I hold up my hand. "Stop right there," I demand, and this time, it's almost a shout. I recognize the intent to kiss me in his eyes and no way am I letting him that close. We need boundaries. Hard, immovable boundaries.

I quickly step around to the other side of the large mahogany conference table. The solid bulk only providing a false sense of security, but I'll take what I can get. Slowly, I pull out one of the leather chairs and sit down, linking my hands before resting them on the table in front of me.

Only then do I look up at Drew, who is still standing, watching me. "Please, sit down, Drew."

He retakes his seat, which puts him directly in front of me, and his eyes lock with mine. I quickly look away. "Why are you here today? Jackie isn't in the office, but I'm sure Laura, my personal assistant, will be able to book you an appointment for tomorrow or the day after. You can see her on your way out."

"Katie, I didn't come to see Jackie. I came to see you." My mouth drops open.

My hands squeeze tightly together, the only physical sign of the tension in my body and the only way I can stop them from visibly shaking. "Why would you want to see me? We have nothing to discuss … I'm not involved in the arrangements for your book tour."

"Aye, I understand Jackie is handling everything regarding promotions, and she's doing a good job. However, I have a special request for the boss … which would be you." He smiles at me. I wish he wouldn't. He looks too damn good. He's put on some weight since I last saw him, and it's obviously been added as toned muscle based on the way he appears to be filling out his shirt.

He leans his elbows on the table in front of him and those muscles strain against the fabric. I wish he'd kept the jacket on, which is currently tossed across the back of a chair beside him. I don't need to be noticing the way his fitted, pale-blue button-up shirt stretches across his upper body and shoulders like a second skin.

"Fine, Drew." I look down at my watch. "But I only have ten minutes before I have to be at a *scheduled* meeting."

"Plenty of time." He's grinning now, and I have no idea why. Honestly, it's making me feel very uncomfortable about what might come next.

He leans back in his seat, stretching his arms up above his head, like he has all the time in the world. I wasn't lying about having a meeting in ten minutes. He doesn't have to know it's only a virtual meeting and I'm an optional attendee, so I can easily skip out. But I'm choosing not to.

I tilt my head to the side. "Maybe this was all you had on your schedule today, but I'm a busy woman. I don't have time to be sitting around pandering to one difficult author."

He sits up straighter and leans toward me again. "I'm not going to do the national book signing tour."

"What? You have to," I stutter in shock. Jackie has spent weeks putting together a comprehensive two-week book signing tour that covers the major cities up and down the country and includes a couple of television interviews.

He shakes his head, and he looks deadly serious now. "I've reviewed the schedule that Jackie sent through, and it's too much."

"Drew, it clearly states in your contract that you're obligated to do all promotional events organized by Carlson Publishing, within reason. Ten events over the two-week period isn't an unreasonable ask." I ensure my tone is firm and professional, but it's hard to keep out the bitchiness I'm feeling.

His brow draws down. "Katie, you know my feelings about public events." He's right, I do, but this is business. I cross my arms over my chest and shrug my shoulders. I don't trust myself to remain firm on this point.

His voice is gravelly and harsh when he says, "I'm prepared to negotiate. If I have to do the national book signing tour, then I'm only available for one week, and I'll only do five signings, one television appearance, and one radio interview."

"Ten days, not seven, and then I think we can work with that," I reply, not missing a beat. It's not unusual to adjust the schedule following discussions with the author.

Then he drops a bombshell. "And you have to do it with me," he adds with a smug smile. What the hell?

I jump up from my seat and brace my hands on the table. "Don't be ridiculous." My voice rises as I continue. "I don't have time for another of your ridiculous demands that serves no purpose other than to boost your ego."

He's back to grinning. "I'd be disappointed if you agreed straight away. But, Katie, so we're clear … that's my final offer if you want me to do this tour."

I stare angrily at him, and unfortunately, I flinch first when I drop back into my chair.

"Why?" I ask softly, all fight in me gone.

"Because we're not done yet, Katie," he replies.

"You had your chance, Drew, and you blew it." I stand up again, and this time, I walk toward the door.

But before leaving, I turn back to him. "And you're wrong. We are done." Then I walk away from him.

Back in the privacy of my office, my shoulders sag under my tailored jacket, and I'm no longer the strong, independent, professional woman. I've become the age-old cliché of a woman falling too hard for a guy who wants nothing more serious than a few nights with her in his bed.

FOURTEEN

Drew

Bollocks. That didn't go the way I'd hoped.

I guess if I was honest with myself, I'd say I couldn't stay away from her, and I was looking for any excuse to see Katie on my first visit to London since the accident. What surprised me was the frosty reception I got.

I didn't expect to be welcomed with open arms, a passionate kiss, and sex on the conference room table, but the *stop right there, don't come another step closer* warning wasn't expected either.

A discussion about the book tour was the reason I planned on using to drop in without a scheduled meeting. I had every intention of negotiating the date changes with Jackie next week. After all, she's in charge of marketing and promotions, not Katie. But when I was met with Katie's hostility, the bullshit just flew out of my mouth before I could think to stop it.

Katie just made it very obvious she doesn't want anything to do with me. I rub my hands across my eyes, trying to work out what happens next. I'm not sure if there is a next move though. What the hell did she mean when she said I blew my chances? I didn't even realize I'd been given a chance. I thought Cornwall was just bad timing for us. My lack of relationship experience puts me at a complete disadvantage. I've never been in a long-term, serious relationship, and it's clear I have no idea how to navigate my way through even a discussion with a woman I'd like to take to dinner.

I've been so buried in my writing and recovery that it never occurred to me she wouldn't want to see me. My few days with Katie in Cornwall seemed to reset what I felt I'd lost with the accident. It unleashed a writing frenzy, and I spent hours every day at my laptop. The only real breaks in those first months after she left were Sean's torture sessions every couple of days.

Slowly, the pain receded enough for me to stop taking the medications completely, my muscles grew stronger, and I no longer needed the crutches. When I could walk unaided, I introduced a beach walk every day. Eventually, some of those walks became runs. Then, last week, for the first time since the accident, I managed to do a three-mile run. It felt good knowing that the slight limp I will be left with is not going to prevent me from doing all the things I love.

A feeling of wholeness is what brought me to London and to Katie's conference room. I guess it's going to take a lot more than that to get Katie to go to dinner with me. I leave the conference room, stopping at her personal assistant's desk on my way out.

"Hello again, Laura. Ms. Carlson suggested you could schedule a meeting with her and Jackie next week."

"Of course, let me just check the meeting calendars." While I wait, I pull my phone from my pocket and bring up my own calendar.

I was planning on staying with Aaron for the next three days before driving up to Scotland to see my family. I'll be having a family Christmas with my mom and siblings. I can delay a few more days if it means I'll see Katie again.

"Mr. Campbell, is Monday at eleven okay?" I check my phone and add the date and time.

"Aye that's fine. I'll look forward to seeing them both then."

"Sorry, but only Jackie will be available to meet with you. Ms. Carlson is flying to New York on the weekend and won't be back until early January." Well, that's an interesting piece of information. I thank Laura and leave.

Two days is not long enough for me to fix what is clearly broken with Katie before she leaves. I did this to her. I made her hate me by pushing her away in Cornwall. Guilt stabs me like a sharp knife thrust into my ribs, and I run my fingers through my hair, trying to figure out how I'm going to make things right.

I look down at my phone and swipe to the last message I sent to Aaron.

Me: *Can you meet me at the Broadway pub at six? I think I've fucked up with Katie.*

Aaron: *Sure. And why am I not surprised you fucked up with a woman?*

I ignore his jibe. I'll save my response for when I see him in an hour and forty minutes. Aaron's not exactly a relationship guru, but he's the only option I've got to help me sort this mess out.

Maybe between us we can come up with something that might result in me getting a second chance with the woman who inhabits my dreams on a nightly basis. My spur-of-the-moment idea of forcing her to join me for the book tour was a shit one, given the look on her beautiful face. The combination of shock, disgust, and sadness all rolled into a storm of emotion swept over her features before she could mask it. I wanted to snatch the words back.

But it was too late. The damage was done.

***

I'm early to meet Aaron, so it's not surprising he isn't waiting for me when I push through the heavy wood and glass door of the pub. We've spent many nights over the years sitting on the same old wooden stools pushed up to the permanently sticky wooden bar, talking or just drinking our pints in silence. Aaron's place is just around the corner, and this has been our pub from the first day he moved in about five years ago.

I don't travel to London often, but when I do, I like to spend as little time as possible amongst the city crowds. I've always preferred the quieter local pubs like the Broadway rather than the ones on the high street.

I order a pint of the locally brewed craft beer they have on tap and settle onto one of our usual stools. The beer arrives with another splash of froth to the bar, and I eagerly bring it to my lips. The cold liquid going down my throat immediately relieves the tension permeating every cell in my body.

It's always the same when I'm in a confined space like a train with a bunch of strangers pressed up against me. The push and shove of people as they fight for the few vacant seats. The lights flickering brightly on, then off again while the tube train speeds through the deep tunnels of the underground, then slowing, threatening to stop due to a signal failure or something on the tracks. It's a terrifying scenario, otherwise known as peak hour on the underground. I could never do this on a regular basis. Maybe I should have had a couple of pints before getting on the tube rather than at the other end.

Unlike some of my former teammates, I don't suffer from full-blown panic attacks in crowded places, but it still makes my palms sweat and my heart pound, and I end up holding myself so rigid that my muscles ache under the stress. I don't belong in the city. I need open spaces with views to the horizon, like my house on the Scottish coastline or, more recently, the rental in Cornwall.

Another few gulps of my beer, and I've completely recovered. Minutes later, Aaron strides through the door. He's a big dude, and in his custom-tailored suit, he tends to draw all the attention in a room. A couple of girls sitting at one of the tables running along the back wall track his progress. He doesn't turn his head, but I know he's noticed them. Aaron never misses the ladies.

He pulls up the stool beside me. "Awrite! How's it gaun?" Aaron still speaks with a heavy accent, the same way he did as a kid, and it's a complete contradiction to the way he looks these days, the professional lawyer. I've had to adjust my accent, words, and phrases for my writing, and it's only when I'm with Aaron or my family that I tend to slip back.

"Hi! I'm fair trashed." He looks my way and nods. I expect I look as exhausted as I feel. Aaron grabs the bartender's attention and orders himself a pint. While he waits, he scans the room. Just like me, he still needs to check out everyone and everything in the near vicinity. Patrols along the dirty, dusty streets of Iraq taught us the hard way to never assume a place is safe.

When the pint comes, he turns to me. "Talk to me. How'd you fuck up with yer woman?" I suck down some more beer, then launch into telling him about my meeting with Katie.

By the time I've finished, he's shaking his head and grinning. "For a clever guy, you're a fucking idiot. Forcing her to see you is never going to work."

"No shit."

"Hey, as my mum always says, failing means yer playing!" It's true. I might be making a mess of everything with Katie, but at least I'm trying.

Aaron finishes the last of his beer and puts the glass back on the bar with a thump. "Let me think on it while you get us another couple of pints. I do my best thinking when I'm steaming." I smile at the absurdity. When Aaron is drunk, he's as much of a fucking idiot as me.

"Thanks, pal."

This is how our friendship has always been. We lean on each other when needed, no questions asked.

FIFTEEN

Katie

Landing back in the States brings a sense of peace. It's good to be home again. While there was no longer a need to travel back earlier to avoid Drew, I decided to keep to my new itinerary rather than change my flights again. With an ocean between Drew and myself, even for only a few weeks, my steps already feel lighter as I gather up my belongings and file out of first class along the corridor to the terminal. I walk faster, knowing Logan will be waiting to meet me on the other side of immigration. Logan, or Logi Bear, the childhood nickname he hates everyone calling him except me, is the brother I've spent the most time with.

Naturally thrown together within the family, being the same age and in the same grade at school, he became one of my best friends. In those early years, we would tell people we were twins, which was totally ridiculous with his fair hair and blue eyes and my completely opposite dark hair and brown eyes. But in our hearts, it's how we saw each other.

I always thought it was cool having a brother in my class, and I would often drag him into whatever crazy new scheme Sarah, Allie, and I had cooked up. The Carlson boys had a reputation for being some of the biggest guys in school, so nobody dared mess with me. But where Hunter and Blake have always loved being the center of attention, Logan shied away from it. He has always been the quiet one of the family. Or, as Blake likes to say, the grumpy, moody one. I don't agree. Logan is a deep thinker who prefers a quiet night in to big social events and likes to bury himself neck deep in the latest financial figures for Carlson Publishing.

I've missed his easy company. It's been too many months since I was home to visit my family. I've seen Hunter during his visits to London over those months, and Logan came once, but otherwise, it was April at my parents' anniversary party when we were all together last.

Christmas is for families, and I wouldn't want to be anywhere else at this time of the year. Next week is the Carlson Christmas Charity Gala and marks the beginning of our family celebrations. This is a special family event, and with all the extended Carlson clan attending, no one would dare miss it. Not that I would want to anyway, because it's always lots of fun. Who wouldn't want to dress up in a beautiful evening gown and drape themselves in diamonds?

Traveling first class means you get to disembark first and your luggage comes through quickly. Twenty minutes after landing, I'm exiting through security and scanning the waiting groups of people for Logan. My three brothers are all around six foot five, so it's never hard to find one of them when they stand taller than most in the crowd. I spot Logan standing to the side, his hands pushed deep into his pockets. I smile at the sight of him. I know I'm not supposed to have a favorite brother, but I guess I just might.

I rush at him, throwing my arms around his neck. He hugs me lightly, and when I step back, his mouth cracks into one of his rare smiles. It warms my heart to see it.

"I've missed you, Kitty Kat." I love hearing him call me by my childhood nickname.

"I've missed you too, Logi Bear." My greeting is accompanied by a punch to his arm—another carryover from our childhood.

He rubs his arm dramatically, like he's been hit by Mike Tyson rather than someone who only reaches to his shoulder.

I laugh. "Come on, let's go. I'm so excited to see Mom and Dad." Hooking my arm through his, I wait for him to lead the way. My rapid-fire questions about family and friends form the soundtrack as we walk to his car and continue through the first ten minutes of our drive into Manhattan.

When a comfortable silence falls between us, I look out the window. It's a cold, blustery day—not surprising, given we're only ten days away from Christmas. I hope it means snow is coming.

***

The next day in the office, the executive team of Carlson Publishing is gathered around the conference table. The team is made up of predominantly family members. Logan is beside me, and across from us are Hunter and my dad. Then at the end is my dad's older brother, Bob, and his son, Jason, who is head of marketing. My dad and Uncle Bob aren't as actively involved in the company's day-to-day workings since they both recently retired, but as board members, they continue to be a part of the quarterly progress meetings and today's end of year reports.

The only person around the table who isn't a family member is Dana, the head of human resources. She joined the firm about two years ago, and she's been a great addition to the team. She has a vibrant personality with a kick-ass can-do attitude and is a lot of fun on a girls' night out. I learned that the hard way. The hangover after our last night out was a bitch.

For the first time as CEO, Hunter kicks off the end of year updates with a short thank-you speech to the group. It's hard to believe it's been nearly a year since Dad handed over the reins to him. He's transitioned into the role so smoothly. The only glitch has been his checking up on me. That has been a pain in the butt, although not unexpected when I know it comes from a good place. I hope that by this time next year, he'll no longer feel the need to take on everyone's problems as his own.

Next to speak is Logan, who provides everyone with a financial update. Dad and Uncle Bob are smiling ear to ear as he rattles off figures, confirming this year has seen a significant increase in profits. Hunter directs us one after the other to provide an update. Each of us sings the praises of our teams, highlighting our achievements, and patting ourselves on the back. It's clear that everyone has contributed to the company's success.

When it gets to me, my update focuses on the new business growth in the UK. I recap on the award as a major achievement and the significant new authors we signed. I attempt to casually rattle off the list of names, and I think I manage it with only a brief mention of Drew.

But just when I think I'm moving on, Hunter looks up from his laptop where he's been typing notes. "Well done, Katie, on signing A.V. Campbell. That was a tough one." He looks back down again briefly, then back up, as if he just remembered something. "Do you know whether he's coming to the Christmas gala?"

My pen clatters to the table, my fingers giving up their tight grip. I watch it roll to the edge and drop to the floor. Bending slowly to retrieve it, I hope this will give me a brief chance to mask my features. If nothing else, at least dropping my head down will give me an excuse to use for my pink cheeks.

"Sorry about that." I flick my hair back from my face and look at Hunter with as much composure as I can muster. "I didn't realize he was invited."

Hunter frowns back at me. "We always invite our top ten authors." He continues to stare at me like I've just grown a second head. Everyone's eyes are now on me. Damn Drew and the hold he has over me.

"Yes, of course. I just hadn't thought he was a top ten. I mean, he only signed with us six months ago." I need to stop talking because I'm just digging the hole I find myself in deeper. "I'll check and let you know."

My heart is racing in my chest like it wants to jump right out and bounce across the table like one of those small wind-up toys we had as children.

I take a sip of water, easing my suddenly dry throat and look down at my laptop, focusing on the words on the screen and picking up where I left off in my update. Somehow, I manage to get the remaining points out. This is my chance to showcase all the good work my team has been doing in the London office, and I don't want thoughts of Drew sabotaging my presentation.

The meeting drags on, and while there are no more awkward questions, it's another hour before we're done. Not soon enough for me. Hunter and Dad stand first, and I slowly pack up my laptop, hoping they'll leave before me. I get the feeling Hunter has some follow-up questions for me.

Dana comes to stand beside me, leaning against the table so her back is to the doorway where the others have congregated. "Are you okay?" she whispers.

"I'm okay, but if you're free tonight, come over to Allie's place for a girls' night, and I'll fill you in on the latest." I keep my voice low, hoping no one will notice the conspiratorial way we're acting.

"Deal. Is seven okay?" she asks, pushing back up to standing.

I agree and pick up my bag. We walk out together, chatting about the weather, of all things. This morning, I woke to a light dusting of snow. It wasn't enough to cover the sidewalks, but the crisp, cold air added to the festive atmosphere in the city.

"I hope the snow means a white Christmas; I love …" My voice falters when I catch sight of Hunter.

Unfortunately, when he left the room, he didn't get as far as his office. Hunter is now standing a little along the corridor, talking to Logan. When I draw level, he says, "Katie, do you have a minute?" I try to gauge from his tone if he's asking as CEO of Carlson Publishing or as my big brother.

"Sure. See you later, Dana." Dana waves her hand, and then she and Logan walk toward the offices at the far end of the corridor. I turn and follow Hunter into his corner office.

A privilege that comes with the weight of responsibility of the CEO role is the biggest, most elaborate office. He's redecorated. When my dad inhabited the space, it had dark-blue walls and a large, rich mahogany desk and bookcase dominating the room. Very traditional. Now it's barely recognizable as the same space with a light woodgrain accent wall and desk mixed with white and charcoal-gray soft furnishings. Several pieces of original abstract artwork cover the walls that aren't floor-to-ceiling glass. Together, it all creates a modern, inviting feel.

I wander over to the windows, remembering the times as kids when Logan and I would come in to visit Dad at the office. We would pretend we were executives. I guess our roles in the company were inevitable, and now we get to live our dreams.

I turn to face Hunter. "I like the new office. It's very different from what Dad had. It suits you."

"Thanks. Dad's desk and bookcase have been moved to his

home office." He smiles at me, then sits in the large leather chair behind the imposing desk and gestures for me to take one of the visitor's chairs. This looks like it's going to be a business discussion.

We only saw each other briefly when I first arrived this morning because he was running late for a meeting. Normally, I love catching up with Hunter, but not today. He seems unhappy about something, and I wonder if there is any way he could have discovered my connection to Drew.

As is Hunter's style, he doesn't waste any time getting to the point. "Is there something I need to know about A.V. Campbell?" Damn him and his perception.

"No, because it's nothing I can't handle," I answer quickly, trying to keep my emotions out of my voice.

It's a few minutes before he speaks again. "I guess that's all I need to know, then." I expect my brush-off has not convinced him, but this time, he's not questioning my ability to handle it.

"Thanks for trusting me. Hey, are you okay? You look exhausted." He looks like he's carrying the weight of the world on his shoulders. I don't remember ever seeing him this down before.

He sighs loudly. "It's been a tough few weeks."

"Tough as in work or something else?" *Or someone*, I think but don't say. I remember him mentioning that he was seeing Trudy, the accountant at Blake's company. It seemed to be getting serious.

"Nothing I can't handle," he replies with a faint smile that doesn't reach his eyes. Parroting my words back to me tells me all I need to know. His problem is woman related, and he knows there's something going on between Drew and me.

I stand up. "If you want to talk, you know where I am."

When we were kids, Hunter was always the big brother I ran to in tears when I was scared of monsters under my bed. He would stomp into my room and shout loudly to tell them to clear off. Then he would let me sleep in the spare bed in his room, reading me one of my princess stories until I fell back to sleep. He has always been our protector, and I'd like to be able to help him for once.

I'll speak to Blake to see if he knows what's up. He and Hunter are very close, being only two years apart in age. Also, Blake's new girlfriend, Bec, is best friends with Trudy. They're bound to know why Hunter seems so down.

SIXTEEN

Katie

It started snowing lightly again on the walk back to my apartment. Well, it was my apartment up until I moved to London. Now it's where Allie is living, across the hall from Logan. It's not a long walk but far enough for the cold air to seep into my lungs and permeate my bones. By the time I reach my building, I'm shivering.

Taking my old key out of my bag, I slip it in the lock. Out of habit, I throw my keys onto the hall table beside Allie's set. Good, she's home already, so we can order food right away. I'm starving.

Walking into the living area, I hear Allie in the kitchen and turn to find her standing next to Logan. They're both staring at me, mouths open, arms hung loosely at their sides. What the hell did I just interrupt? They couldn't look guiltier if they tried.

"Logan, I wasn't expecting to see you tonight." I can't hide my smirk.

He shuffles his feet back and forth, just like he used to do as a kid when Dad caught us sneaking Twinkies from the cupboard before dinner. What have I missed between Logan and Allie while I've been caught up in my own Drew drama? Damn, first Hunter, and now Logan. I'm so out of the family loop.

"Just leaving, Katie," he says, quickly disappearing in the direction of the door before I have a chance to ask one of the many questions springing to mind. Huh, Logan may have escaped my questioning, but Allie is still here, and I turn toward her with my arms folded.

"Okay, spill. What the hell is going on with you and Logan?"

She shakes her head. "It's complicated, like our 'friendship' has always been," she says, gesturing in quotes around the word friendship. Then, pretending to be busy, she wipes down the granite countertop that's already spotless before throwing the cloth back in the sink. "Anyway, we're not here to talk about me. You need to fill me in on the latest with Drew."

I place the bottle of Moet I brought home with me on the countertop between us. "Okay. You pour the bubbles while we wait for Dana. She was just finishing a call as I was leaving the office, so she should be here soon. I'm going to change into something more comfortable really quick." I look down at the red silk pajama pants covered in snowmen and candy canes that Allie is wearing. "Though not something like those," I tell her, laughing. "Seriously, it's hard to understand how you can be part of the fashion industry when you're wearing those."

"Hey, don't throw shade on my snowmen," she says, glancing down with a huge smile on her face. "Wait till you see the green elf pair I'm saving for Christmas Day. They're even cuter."

"Whatever you say. You're the expert." Laughing loudly, I wander down the hall to the spare bedroom to change.

By the time I've pulled on black leggings and my super-soft, striped cashmere sweater, I'm all set for our girls' night in. Dana has arrived, and both of my friends are sitting on the sofa, discussing food options. Personally, I don't care what they order, as long as it comes quickly. I'm not a fussy eater, and I missed lunch today. My stomach growls, emphasizing the fact that I need food.

Allie hands me a glass of champagne, and I curl my feet under me as I sit in the single chair opposite them. Dana finishes placing the order, and my stomach rumbles louder at the prospect of all that deliciousness coming my way soon.

"Food should be here in fifteen minutes," Dana announces, throwing her cell on the cushion beside her before picking up her glass and raising it up. "Cheers, girls. To another year of kicking career goals, ditching crap boyfriends, and the best friends a girl can have."

"Oh, hun, that is so sweet." We all clink our glasses together, then take a sip. The fizz and pop of the cold bubbles are perfect for our catch-up. And Dana wastes no time in getting us started.

"Katie, I've been dying to find out what the latest with Drew is. Obviously something has happened based on the meeting this morning."

I tap my hand to my head, groaning. "Please don't remind me. I guess I didn't do a very good job of hiding my horror at finding out Drew was invited to the gala. It's even worse than that though because I called my promotions manager right after and she told me he accepted."

"Whoa, wait. I have no idea what you girls are talking about," Allie complains, looking between Dana and me. "Can you start at the beginning, please? This sounds juicy."

I take another fortifying sip of champagne, then begin. "Okay, but I'll go back to last week when he showed up unexpectedly in the office. I'd heard nothing from him for months—not a call or a text, absolutely nothing—then he just showed up asking to see me."

Allie interrupts me with a hissed "Bastard."

"Asshole," Dana concurs.

"Absolutely," I agree wholeheartedly, then continue to fill them in on the meeting I had with Drew only five days ago. I still can't believe he didn't mention the invitation once during the meeting. I end my story with a recap for Allie of how I found out he'd been invited to the gala at this morning's executive meeting.

"Damn, so he's going to be there," Allie confirms. I nod, feeling the weight of her words pulling my shoulders down. I was worried about seeing him for the book signing in January, but now I'm going to have to see him in three days instead of next month. And I can't avoid it. The family-sponsored Christmas charity gala is a big deal, and attendance by the family is expected.

Allie jumps up from the sofa, a splash of champagne from the glass in her hand landing on the coffee table. "There's only one thing you can do!" she announces, almost bouncing on her feet with excitement. I'm surprised more champagne isn't spilling over. Not that I'd care if she spilled the whole glass at this point, because I'm more worried about what she's about to say.

Over the years, I've learned that when Allie gets this excited about something, trouble soon follows. Like the time she decided we should go skinny-dipping at midnight in the ocean at the beach house and my three brothers discovered us. Or the time she decided we should sneak some of her parents' vodka before going to Logan's sixteenth birthday party, and I ended up throwing up in the bathroom, missing the party completely.

Reluctantly, I ask, "What do you have in mind?"

"Revenge," she announces while rubbing her hands together.

My brows draw down in confusion. "Revenge for what?"

"For him not realizing how totally awesome you are when he had the chance. And for seducing you with his dick sorcery."

I laugh. "Thanks, girlfriend. Not that I know what dick sorcery even is … and maybe we can dial back a little on the revenge idea."

Allie shrugs her shoulders, then flops back onto the sofa. Luckily, this time her glass is safely on the coffee table. "Fine, but I'm still going to get you the most stunning dress that will have him choking on his canapes. I have the perfect dress for you. It's by a new designer, and I wore it at her runway show last week."

Allie has the best contacts in the fashion industry and excellent taste when it comes to choosing outfits for me, Christmas pajamas being the only obvious exception.

"Now that's the kind of idea I can get on board with."

"Will she have something for me too?" Dana asks sheepishly. "I haven't had time to go shopping for my dress either."

Allie reaches out to tap Dana's hand. "Absolutely. I'll text her now and see if we can drop into her studio tomorrow. Is that okay? Jules, the designer, only has two seamstresses, so they'll need a day or two for minor alterations." Then, shaking her head, she reprimands us. "Why do you girls always leave things to the last minute?"

Dana laughs. "Because our lives don't revolve around what we wear. A wardrobe of classic basics is generally all I need." Dana offers up as an excuse, and Allie's response is to scrunch her face in horror. Even pulling a face, she still manages to look as beautiful as she does on the covers of the glossy magazines.

The intercom buzzes, and Allie gets up to answer it. I expect—no, I hope—that the call from the doorman is to tell us the food is here. The second glass of champagne is going straight to my head with an empty stomach.

Food arrives and another bottle of champagne is opened. Our girls' night in soon descends into a giggle fest.

I do miss these nights since moving to London, but I guess when we do get to catch up, it does make them more special.

***

At the Carlson Christmas Charity Gala

Placing my hand on my stomach, I hope to settle the nerves that are break dancing there and threatening to reject the salmon canape I stupidly popped in my mouth. A quick scan of the smattering of guests that have arrived early confirms that Drew is not here yet.

I wish I could sneak away from where I'm standing with Logan and Allie just inside the entrance of the grand ballroom. However, Mom and Dad expect the family to be available to greet guests not far from the entrance, so I'm stuck, my eyes darting left and right, expecting Drew to walk through the door at any moment.

Usually, I don't mind this part of the evening. In fact, I enjoy welcoming people, and I'm proud to stand beside my parents and brothers. We've been a close-knit unit ever since I joined the Carlson clan. The idea of three instant big brothers was initially daunting for seven-year-old me, but eventually, with Hunter's encouragement, we all slotted in together, like pieces in a puzzle.

This is my home turf, which makes the possibility of seeing Drew feel more personal. Up to this point, Drew has been compartmentalized in my mind away from my real life.

Thirty minutes later, the family duty part of the evening is done. I run my hands over the smooth forest-green silk crepe fabric that hugs my body—my so-called revenge dress. In my mind, it's less revenge and more elegantly simple. The only adornment is a band of beading edging the deep V between my breasts and on the thin straps over my shoulders. But my favorite part of the dress is the completely open back. This dress is all about drawing the observer's eye to key areas, my cleavage and my butt.

Unfortunately, or maybe fortunately at this point, it has all been for nothing, because there is still no sign of Drew. Maybe he decided not to come after all. We move toward the bar area, but every so often, I glance back to the entrance. Even from this distance, I still can't settle into enjoying the evening. The glass of champagne clasped tightly in my fist isn't releasing the tension in my body either. I can't remember the last time I was this nervous.

I look down, realizing the glass I've been holding is empty. I'm not sure when that happened, but as a waiter passes nearby, I grab his attention to trade my empty one for a full one. With the cold liquid fizzing on my tongue, I glance again to the entrance, and there he is. I nearly spit my drink back into the glass.

Until this moment, I couldn't believe he would come. Mostly because I can't imagine the reason why.

Allie follows my gaze and nudges my arm. "Is that him? Holy hell, his hotness is burning my retinas."

Logan glares at her with his classic, well-rehearsed grumpy face in place. "Seriously? You're here to meet the guests, not drool all over their tuxedos."

"And you're here to not be an asshole, Logan," she quips, rolling her eyes, then turning slightly away from him.

"I'm going to get another drink," Logan announces before storming off.

"Whoa, you two are sounding toxic. Whatever is going on with you guys lately, you need to sort it out."

"Let's just forget about him, because I think your scorching-hot author dude needs your attention. Wow, he is one fine-looking specimen of a man. You should go talk to him before someone else does. Go on." Allie nudges me in Drew's direction.

Spinning on my black satin Jimmy Choo sandals, I demand, "Are you insane?" Did she not listen to a word I said the other night about my feelings around Drew? Was I not clear that I'm hopeless at resisting him whenever he's nearby? Why on earth would I want to go talk to him?

Before I can say more, Logan returns, looking like he's seen a ghost. "What's up?" I ask, glad for the distraction.

"The guy who was going to be the silent auction prize is a no-show, and Dad wants me to do it." Allie bursts out laughing, drawing one of Logan's infamous glares. Every year, one of the silent auction prizes has been a dinner date with one of Manhattan's most eligible bachelors. Hunter and Blake have stepped up to do this in the last couple of years, but Logan has always managed to avoid it.

"You have to bid on me, Kitty Kat." Poor Logan. I imagine he sees this as his worst possible nightmare.

"I can't bid on you; you're my brother. But Allie can." We both turn to look at her.

She holds her hands up. "Why on earth would I want to pay for a date with him?" Logan's mouth drops open, but no words come out.

"Allie, be nice," I warn. "Logan will pay you back, and you don't actually have to go on the date."

"Please, Allie. Just this one thing is all I need," he begs, and the fact that he's asking shows his desperation. I've never heard him ask Allie for anything in all the years they've known each other.

She folds her arms across her chest. "Fine, I'll do it. But you owe me." Logan nods his head sharply once.

"Yeah, okay. But can we please just get your bid submitted now?" They wander off in the direction of the silent auction tables.

During Logan's little drama, I lost track of Drew. I search the crowd gathered near the entrance, but I can't see his dark head.

If he's not there, where is he?

SEVENTEEN

Drew

With another tug on my bow tie, I look around the fancy ballroom. There are a lot of people here, but luckily it's a huge ballroom, so I'm not feeling stressed. No, tonight the tension in my body is completely unrelated to crowds of people. I'm so out of place amongst all these rich socialites and this tuxedo has me feeling trussed up like a Christmas turkey. In my head I congratulate myself on the analogy since it feels like I've just stepped into the fire.

I wonder again if Katie knows I'm coming tonight. She didn't mention it the other day in the London office, so maybe she doesn't even know I've been invited.

I shove one hand deep into the pocket of my trousers and with the other, take a glass of champagne off the tray of a passing waiter. I wish I didn't feel like a stray dog that's wandered into a cattery. You don't get a lot of Christmas charity galas where I grew up, so who knows what even goes on at one.

With another glance about the room from my new vantage point, I spot her talking to a big guy and a statuesque brunette in red. It's hard to tell if the guy is with Katie or the woman in red until suddenly, the man and woman walk away, leaving Katie alone.

I approach her from behind, and when I'm within arm's reach, I say in a low voice, "Good evening, Katie."

She jumps, champagne from her nearly full glass, spilling onto her finger. She turns slowly. "Drew."

The sound of my name on those sweet red lips is like a siren song, and I want her right here, right now. Except we're standing in the middle of a ballroom filled with people.

Her eyes flash with fire, and it's the only warning I get before she says through clenched teeth, "Why are you here?" Okay, she's pissed. This time, I was expecting her anger. It would have been stupid to think otherwise after our meeting last week.

I take a step back. "I was invited." She's not surprised to see me, so my answer should be expected.

She rolls her eyes, then hisses, "Yes, but why did you come? Wasn't it less publicity you were looking for last week?"

I like this fired-up version of Katie. She's got claws, and it's sexy as hell.

"I came to see you. After our meeting, I didn't expect I'd be granted another opportunity to speak to you." It's an honest response, but from her pained expression, it's not exactly welcome.

She closes her eyes briefly as she draws in a deep breath. Then she speaks like each word is coated in spikes. "Just stop. You run hot and cold depending on the day … or your mood … Playing your little games with me like I'm your latest shiny toy. I don't like it, and

I want you to stop."

I reach out to hold her hand, the one she was just waving at me. "I don't mean to—"

But before I can finish, a giant of a man strides up to us and interrupts. "What the hell is going on here?" he demands, and as he stares at our clasped hands, Katie quickly withdraws hers from mine.

She spins, placing herself partially between me and the intruder. "It's okay, Hunter. Have you met Drew, also known as A. V. Campbell?" She looks over her shoulder at me. "Drew, this is Hunter Carlson, CEO of Carlson Publishing."

Fuck. It hits me; this is one of Katie's stepbrothers, which is why he's gone all protective intimidation on me.

I stretch out my hand to him. "Hunter." He takes it in a firm, viselike grip while continuing to look between Katie and me. Well, this isn't exactly a stellar introduction to her family, especially since I couldn't resist responding to Hunter's grip with one of my own, making it a pissing competition. There's no winner, but I think we understand each other better. At six foot three, I'm tall and obviously know how to take care of myself, but even I would think twice about taking this guy on. He's huge. If all of her brothers are like this one, then it's a wonder anyone ever dared to ask her on a date.

Then, as if I've conjured up the complete Carlson clan, two other dudes of equal height join us, flanking Hunter. What the fuck?

Katie turns to me again and is now trying unsuccessfully to mask a smile. "Drew, these are my other brothers. Blake." She points to the fairer of the two men standing shoulder to shoulder with Hunter. They must all be at least six foot five. "And this is Logan."

I step forward and shake hands with each of the men, concealing my reaction as first Blake, then Logan each deliver bone-crushing handshakes. They fucking know I've had sex with their sister.

Katie says to Hunter, "Drew and I were just discussing his UK book tour after the new year." Hunter squints, then glares at me. He definitely knows there's something going on here, and I'd say he's not happy about it. I hold his stare.

She continues with inane small talk, and I let her because eventually it has the desired effect of moving her brothers on, one by one. Logan is the last to leave, and as he heads in the direction of the bar, Katie turns to face me.

"I'm sorry about that. No one should have to put up with my ridiculously overprotective brothers. Not even you." She worries her bottom lip, and I want to rub my thumb over it. But I know that wouldn't be welcomed.

"So how many of your brothers know I slept with you?"

Her eyes become huge. "Only Logan definitely … but maybe Blake because his girlfriend, Bec, and I are friends. I may have mentioned something when I spoke to her a couple of weeks ago."

I smile down at her. "Blake knows, if the small broken bones in my hand are anything to go by."

"Sorry again. I know they can be a little intense. At least they didn't ask you to step outside. Logan was always doing that in high school."

"I got the impression Blake was the one to watch. Isn't he former special forces?"

She chokes out a laugh, her first one with me tonight. "Yes, a former Army Ranger."

I smile down at her, enjoying the shift to our lighthearted discussion. "Good to know, and I'm probably lucky I only ended up with a crushed hand."

"Why did you come, Drew?" she asks, placing her hands on her hips. "This better not be a booty call, because that is not happening after our last conversation."

"No booty call unless you ask for one. I promise." Unexpectedly, a fire in the depths of her eyes seems to spark to life. But I've made a promise to her. If anything is going to happen tonight, she will need to instigate it.

"Katie, I came tonight because I wanted to speak to you in private, and like I said before, I figured this was going to be my only opportunity."

She looks around the crowded room. "Seems like you don't have the privacy you hoped for."

"True. Will you come with me somewhere more private? I feel like I'm being watched by your menacing brothers." It's not the complete truth, given I have a good view of the room behind her and can see each of them standing not far away, but they're all busy chatting with groups of other people.

She worries her bottom lip. I'm beginning to realize this means she's undecided about wanting to do something.

She's wavering. "Katie, I might be an arsehole, but I'm also a man of my word. I promise that you hold the control tonight."

I hold my breath, waiting to hear if she is going to give me a chance.

With a roll of her eyes and a flick of an offending piece of hair that's dared to slip forward over her shoulder, she mumbles, "Fine." And the held air escapes from my lungs. I offer her my hand, but she only looks at it, then crosses her arm around her waist.

"Let's go," she says, and accepting her rules of engagement, I follow her through the groups of people toward the entrance, depositing our glasses on a waiter's tray before we exit. I look left and right, then suggest we go down a carpeted hallway with signs leading to additional function rooms. Katie continues to walk beside me, but her silence feels unnatural.

I lead her past the bathrooms, then around a corner to a quieter area. There are three doors leading off the narrower hallway to what I assume is a series of small function or meeting rooms. I try the first door, and surprisingly, it gives under my hand. I open it enough to be able to poke my head through. It's a completely empty, darkened room. Perfect, though I didn't really expect us to find this level of privacy. A smile tips up the corner of my mouth.

I open the door wider. "It's empty. Are you okay with this?" I'm disturbed by her lack of words since we left the ballroom. Katie, in my previous experience, has always chatted, particularly when she gets nervous. It's amazing that after the little amount of time we've spent together I already know this about her. I don't think I've ever paid so much attention to the way a woman moves or her habits. Like chewing her lip or the way her breathing quickens when we stand close, like now. I guess it's because none of those other women captured my attention enough for me to bother.

The beautiful woman beside me has always been different, which is why I'm here in a darkened hotel function room, hoping to say something, anything, to try to get us back to the way we were in Cornwall.

We're standing only a foot apart and her eyes are focused directly on me like she's waiting for me to say more.

Clearing my throat, I begin, "I came to New York because I didn't want to wait another six weeks to see you."

She huffs and drops her gaze. "You didn't seem to have trouble waiting months before showing up at my office last week."

"To be fair, I explained in Cornwall that I wasn't going to be able to get to London. And when I emailed you, it was clear from your response that you probably weren't interested in seeing me."

With one finger, I tip her chin back up to me. The lighting is dim in here, even with the door slightly ajar and a thin strip of light from the hallway bleeding into the darkness. It's enough for me to read the expression in her eyes though. She's not forgiven me for sending her away in Cornwall. I know I fucked up and it's way past time I explained and apologized.

"Katie, I know you hate me for not promising you more after

Cornwall, but I wasn't in a good place then. I was struggling to write and frustrated by the slow progress of my recovery. I'm sorry for handling the situation so badly."

"Hate is a strong word," she says softly, then straightens, seemingly gathering strength before continuing, "What I don't understand is why you coerced me into going all the way down to Cornwall only to reject me when I was there. What was that about? Honestly, I have no idea, because it sure as hell wasn't about getting the contract signed."

"Aye, it had nothing to do with the contract. Like I explained at the time, I wanted to see you to apologize for sneaking away after our night together."

"Fine, so you apologized. But then why did you seduce me with some kind of dick sorcery that had me falling into bed with you? If you were only going to tell me to go home when we were done. It was like, *that was fun, now go back to London.*"

I let my finger drop from under her chin. I want to hold her to me, kiss away the doubt I planted in her. But I can't do any of that because I promised that she had the control.

"There were no plans of seduction involved. You've always been a willing participant. And I don't even know what dick sorcery is, so I'm pretty sure I wasn't doing any of that."

"Oh yes, you were," she states while poking me in the shoulder with one ruby-red painted fingernail. Even her nails shout sex goddess, and a fleeting thought of her wrapping them around my cock has me hardening uncomfortably behind the zipper of my dinner suit. I'm a sick bastard, getting turned on by her anger.

She huffs again, and this time places both hands on her hips. "Like I said before, I'm not your plaything."

Plaything. The word has me conjuring up more images of Katie, naked and sliding down onto my shaft.

I try not to look at the way the fabric of her dress pulls across her beautiful breasts but fail. It's hard not to remember how they spilled out of my palms. How her dusky, sensitive nipples pebbled at my touch.

"Did you check out my tits when I just told you I wasn't your plaything?"

"Sorry. I know I'm a fucking dirty bastard." I add my flirty smile to the words. Not that I suspect Katie is about to fall for it. She's not happy that I'm here, and she's not afraid to let me know.

We engage in a staring contest. No words, just an intense battle of wills encapsulated in a focused look. Her bag slips from her shoulder and drops to the floor with a thud, but we barely acknowledge it. Then, just as I think she's about to send me packing, she surprises me by doing the opposite.

One manicured hand grabs a hold of the lapel of my jacket, and she pulls me to her. Her lips capture mine in a demanding, devouring, hungry kind of kiss that has my cock jumping to attention and my arms folding tightly around her. I flatten my hand on her bare back, and the skin-to-skin contact ratchets up the heat between us. I've been wanting to stroke my hand along the sweep of her back since I first saw her in the smoking-hot dress.

Her hips push flush up against my body. I know she can feel what she's doing to me, and I suspect the power is making her wet. In my experience, Katie doesn't like to hold back her desire.

Briefly, I rip my lips from hers. "Are you wanting more?" We've gone from nought to steamy in the blink of an eye, and I need to be clear on what her end game is.

"Yesss … I need you inside me now," she pants out before reaching for my belt and nimbly unbuckling it. The button is undone next, then the zipper, and then her hand is diving into my boxer shorts. I close my hand around her wrist, halting her.

I groan into the shell of her ear. "You fucking wreck me. So you're going to need to slow down, or this will be over sooner than you want."

Her body seems to comply, and taking both her hands, I drag them above her head, pinning them to the wall within my stronger grip. Her head drops back, and her eyes flutter closed. Elegance and beauty all wrapped up in the way her body arches back. My free hand slips through the high slit in the side of her dress, trailing over the soft skin of her thighs and around to her butt. I give it a squeeze. The moan that slips from her lips is encouraging and sexy as hell. I massage and knead the cheek, all the while trailing kisses along her jawline and up and down her neck, then nuzzling behind her ear. The perfume she obviously dabbed there earlier this evening reminds me of forbidden nights of lust. A bit like us now, hiding here in this room with the potential of being exposed any moment by an overzealous staff member. We probably don't have much time before she's missed from the party.

"Hook your leg on my hip. I need you to open for me." She does exactly as I ask, and when I whisper, "Good girl" into her ear, her body quivers beneath my hand. I capture her lips in a kiss while my hand strokes back over her thigh, then slips into the junction. Her pussy is barely covered by a triangle of satin, and as my fingers reach under the edge, it's damp.

I swipe a finger along her folds. She's dripping wet. Katie wriggles in my arms, urging me to do it again.

"Tell me, baby, what do you want?"

"More … I … just want … more … I always want more." Her voice is husky with need, but there is an edge to it tonight that wasn't there in Cornwall. She still sounds angry, with me or herself, I'm not sure.

My thumb gently circles her clitoris, giving her just a little more. A loud moan escapes her lips, echoing through the room. "Shhh … we don't want to be discovered."

I feed two fingers deep into her swollen channel, and she is instantly writhing in my arms, searching for her release. Her walls hold me tight. She's so close.

The sounds falling from her lips are needy and desperate as she reaches for her release. I rub my thumb rougher over her sensitive bud, then press down firmly. Her high-pitched tweets driving me on to give her what she's begging for as I pump my fingers deeply. I'm loving the sounds of her pleasure.

She falls apart in my arms. "Ahh." She moans out her release, and I drink the sweet sounds into my mouth.

Her wrists strain against my hand as she rides the waves of pleasure.

Her features, which were tense moments ago, soften.

Her eyes, which were squeezed tightly shut, are now fluttering open like she's awoken from a deep slumber.

A vibration comes from her bag on the floor, making it bounce. We both look down at it, but neither of us bends to pick it up.

"Do you want to get that?" I ask, but I already know the answer when she drops her leg down.

She looks at me, and her eyes are filled with regret.

I'm not surprised when she says firmly, "You need to leave now."

EIGHTEEN

Katie

The moment Drew is out the door, I slump back against the wall, then slide slowly down to the floor. I don't even care that sitting on a possibly dirty floor will damage my beautiful designer dress. Instead, I concentrate on catching my breath, slowing my racing heartbeat, and trying to figure out what the hell just happened. Why do I let him do this to me? I know I don't mean anything to him other than a casual hookup, a convenient lay, and I deserve more than that. But the moment our bodies connect, we're combustible. A need so raw and desperate takes me over, and like an addict, I need my fix. A high that only Drew's touch can give me.

My phone vibrates again in my bag beside me, demanding my

attention. I quickly pull it from my evening bag and slide to check my messages.

Allie: *Hey, where did you go? And why aren't you answering your phone?*

Me: *I'm still here, but I need to leave. Like now.*

Allie: *Where is here? Because I haven't been able to find you.*

I send her the directions to my hiding place in the darkened meeting room, and shortly after, I can hear her quietly calling my name from the hallway. Dragging myself up from the floor, I brush off my dress and open the door. The bright light is momentarily blinding as I call to Allie at the end of the corridor.

"Wow, what happened to you? You look like you've just been …" Allie's hand flies to her mouth, and her perfectly arched eyebrows stretch higher than usual.

"Don't even think about finishing that sentence. I don't want to talk about it … yet. Just get me out of here without running into one of my family members." I run my fingers through my tangled, messy hair, which only a half hour ago was softly curled and artfully held in place by firm-hold gel and hairspray. It turns out not even the most expensive hair styling products can withstand thirty minutes under Drew's onslaught.

When I've finished fixing my hair the best I can, I realize Allie is still staring at me, her mouth slightly open.

"Stop looking at me like that. We need to go." And like a starter's gun going off, she springs into action, grabbing me by the hand. With quick, small steps, she drags me down the hallway back toward the ballroom. I trust she knows where she's going, because at this point, I have no idea.

When we're just about back to the hallway where the bathrooms are, she snags the attention of a waiter. Then with a flutter of her lashes, she convinces him to collect our coats from the coat check desk and direct us out through another exit. The concierge hails us a cab, and shortly after, we're on our way home.

Sighing with relief, I glance sideways at my friend. "Thanks, Al, and I'm sorry I dragged you away from the party early."

She turns to face me and reaches out to pat my hand that's resting on the seat between us. "What else are friends for?" Then, in a lowered voice so the driver can't hear, she asks, "Was it more dick sorcery?"

I nod. "Damn that man and his sorcery. He messes with my head and pretty much everything else. I'm better off just not being around him."

"Is he gone?"

I nod again. "I told him to leave … I assume he did." My brow crinkles with the memory of him walking out the door. He didn't object. He just left. I guess it tells me everything I need to know. He got what he wanted tonight. Well, maybe not everything he planned on, because I'm sure he wasn't expecting to be left with blue balls.

With a shake of my head, I try to dislodge the feeling of having been used or, more accurately, letting myself be used. The blame needs to be shared though. I should never have agreed to go somewhere private with him, especially when I know I can't resist his *charms*.

I check my phone, but there's nothing from Drew. Instead, there is a slew of messages from Allie. I scroll through them. "Oh, I missed the silent auction. Did you win Logan?"

She huffs loudly. "Yes, but really, is that winning? Dinner with him is more like a joke prize and certainly not worth the ridiculous bid he made me submit."

"You two really should try to get along better. It's not like you can avoid each other when you're two of my closest people."

Even though she's looking out the window, I can tell by the movement of her shoulders that she just rolled her eyes. That's the thing about best friends: you know all their little gestures, loves, and hates.

Funny thing though, I can't figure out if Logan fits into the love or hate bucket for Allie.

***

Six Weeks Later

I can't believe it's nearly the end of January and I haven't done anything about my New Year's resolutions yet. Maybe this year they're unattainably high goals since I'm going to be turning thirty and I've got big things to get done.

I always expected that by thirty I would have found a special someone to share my life with, and maybe I'd even be contemplating starting a family. I've watched my brothers find love, first Blake with Bec, then recently Hunter with Trudy, and I want some of that for myself. Instead, I'm unhappily single and pining after a man I can't even call my own. Because the only man who has come close to being Mister Right has decided I don't fit into his life plan.

In the early hours of the new year, when I'd drunk too much champagne, resolution number one—to find a man—made sense. Now I'm not so sure. All I know is I don't want a casual relationship. The occasional hookups with Drew is enough for me to know it's not what I want for my future. I want someone who is there for me to talk to when I get home from work, who will comfort me when I'm stressed, who will treat me like a princess at night and embrace my independence during the day.

What's stopping me from putting myself out there and having a crack at finding a new man? It's that I'm still hung up on last year's man, who quite possibly could have been the one.

My other two resolutions were simpler, yet they still remain elusive. Number two was to join the gym near my place in Kensington. It's a little predictable for a resolution, though trying to fit a workout into my busy schedule is proving challenging. And then there was number three. The one goal that I'm making progress with, because it relates to work. I need to grow Carlson Publishing in the UK and Europe to prove to myself that I deserve my place as a senior executive. Some of that growth revolves around the release of Drew's book and the book signing tour of the UK.

Jackie has been able to finalize the dates and locations for the signings with Drew. I open the attachment to the email that just popped up on my laptop. Surprisingly, he's even agreed to do a local morning television interview in Edinburgh. I know Drew hates putting his face out there, but he agreed to do this one if his family and I were there. More demands, but this time it was easy to agree. I planned on being there anyway.

On cue, a text from Drew pops up on my phone screen. I was expecting it because he was sent the same email confirmation from Jackie.

Drew: *Just checking that you'll be at the studio for the Edinburgh television interview on the eighteenth.*

I'm learning that despite his commanding arrogance, underneath the façade is a very private man who hates being the center of attention. One who would rather hide out on an isolated coastline in Cornwall, or anywhere else for that matter, than attend a publicity event. Unfortunately, this is at odds with the profession he chose. Being an author with global success requires marketing yourself to readers.

Me: *Yes, Drew. I'll be there. It's an early start, and I'll be staying in the same hotel the night before.*

Drew: *And the night after.*

I notice his message is a statement, not a question, and my brow creases in annoyance. The man is giving me creases in my forehead I wasn't expecting to have to deal with for at least a few more years.

Me: *I'll have to check my calendar.*

Drew: *You need to be there after the interview too. I want you to meet my family.*

He really needs to learn how to ask, not just demand. Although that probably makes me a hypocrite because I liked his demands in the bedroom. Not that it's appropriate for me to be thinking along these lines while I'm sitting at my desk in my office. I cross my knees, clenching my thighs together and tamping down memories of Drew demanding I strip for him. Focusing back on the text message thread, I reply.

Me: *I'll see what I can do.*

Drew: *Katie ...*

Me: *Drew ...*

This is how our business-related text conversations usually go. Each of us trying to stand our ground as the other attempts to pull in a different direction or, in this case, toward a different arrangement. I thought this was all settled, and I can already feel myself giving into the idea of dinner with Drew and his family.

Drew texts me regularly. Almost daily. The first text was about an hour after he left the gala, asking if I was okay. I appreciated him reaching out, and it avoided future awkwardness when more texts followed. There was one wishing me a happy new year one minute after midnight, and another the day he was having the promotional photos taken. He hated doing that. Then there were others telling me about his day and asking about mine. Sometimes he just asks, "How's it going?" or shares a funny meme or joke. I can see he's making an effort, an olive branch of friendship. The problem I have is that I want more than friendship, which makes just being friends feel impossible.

I'm reminded that there was something I needed to ask him.

Me: *How would you feel about doing a few signings and promotional events in the States?*

I don't have long to wait to see his response.

Drew: *Maybe, but no more television interviews. I'll be in London the night before the book tour begins. Are you free for* *dinner to discuss?*

It's the first time since the gala that he's suggested we meet. The book tour begins next week, and my trepidation is already mounting when I think about seeing him again at the first book signing. We've never been on a date, not that a business discussion over dinner would be a date. Regardless, I'm not sure it's a good idea. I've made some bad decisions when it's come to Drew, and it's time I started making good ones.

Me: *Sorry, I have a lot on my plate because I'll be out of the office for the week. We can talk when I see you at the signing.*

Drew: *Okay, fine.*

I frown at his short response.

An entire week with Drew on his book tour is going to be difficult. Part of me can't wait to see him again, but another bigger part feels like he's the last person I want to spend time with because of the danger he poses to my heart.

After our encounter in New York, I tried to block out the emotional turmoil those moments in his arms cost me. It was easy initially, with all the comings and goings of Christmas with my family, then Blake and Bec getting engaged. But after returning to London, and even more lately, he has been popping into my thoughts way too often.

What's worse are the late nights lying alone in my bed when the memories of his touch come flooding back. Those times are becoming more frequent as the book tour dates loom closer.

In a week, I'll be packing my overnight bag and heading north to Liverpool for the first day of signings. I go back to looking at the schedule on my laptop. The first stop on the first morning will be an hour-long book signing at the flagship store of the national bookstore chain Stones. Then in the afternoon, there is another signing at one of the larger independent bookstores, followed by an interview with a journalist from the local newspaper. I have an early morning meeting in London that day. It finishes at ten, which will give me enough time to drive north for the afternoon signing. I tell myself that it's only five days of the full ten-day schedule that I have to get through. Five days of protecting my heart and avoiding alone time with Drew. I close the document, deciding I have other work to do that does not revolve around Mr. A. V. Campbell.

This whole thing cannot be over soon enough.

NINETEEN

Drew

One Week Later

Day one of the book tour, and the line of readers waiting for their books to be signed snakes between the many tables of stacked books holding all the latest releases categorized into the most popular genres of crime, thriller, biographies, and romance. More books line the walls on shoulder-high bookshelves, row upon row of them, some only showing bindings, while others display eye-catching covers. And there, in the center of this booklover's nirvana, is my book. The angry blood-red slash across the otherwise black-and-white cover is dramatic and hard to ignore. Especially when the high towers of books appear to be surrounding the table I'm sitting at. Well, they were high towers, but slowly, they've been eaten away by the avid readers who are snatching up one or more copies before joining the back of the queue, waiting for their book to be signed.

I look up from the open copy in front of me and smile before handing it over to its new owner. Who'd have thought sitting and signing books would be so exhausting? I surreptitiously look at my watch, then do a quick scan of my surroundings. It's been more than an hour, yet still I can't see the back of the line. I lean toward Jackie, who is acting as my minder today, and ask in a low voice only she can hear, "How much longer?"

"I think we'll do the additional half hour, then call it quits. I just hate to disappoint people when they've been waiting in line," she confirms. I glance back up at the line of people chatting excitedly. She's right; I don't want to disappoint all these people.

"I'm fine to keep going till everyone in the line has their signed copy, but let's get them to stop anymore joining."

Jackie smiles at me. "Thanks, Drew. And it's a nice problem to have." She's right, I've never really had it pointed out to me so obviously how popular my books are. Sure, the seven-figure royalties payment arrives monthly, and that tells me how successful my earlier releases have been, but still, the magnitude has never really sunk in. Maybe this book tour isn't going to be as bad as I thought it would be. Now I only need Katie to turn up, and then I'll feel even better.

We've been messaging regularly over the last month, but since our disastrous last meeting at the Christmas gala in New York, I haven't seen her. I've wanted to ask her on a date, but each time I was about to, something came up. Then, the one time I did go into the office to meet with Jackie, she happened to be away at some meeting. I figured she was avoiding me, so I didn't bother making the trip up from Cornwall again.

I know I've still got some work to do with Katie if she's to forgive me for pushing her away. I thought that explaining why would repair the damage, but I guess she needs more. I didn't realize exactly how much I'd hurt her until New York. Now I'm going to have to prove to her that I'm not the callous playboy she initially took me for. I have to win her trust, because I'd like to see where this could go between us.

This book signing tour is probably my last chance to show her that I don't see her as just my plaything, like she accused. Maybe in the past I could have been called out for treating women as casual flings, though I was always clear that I wasn't looking for anything more, but not Katie. Since the very first kiss, and that first night in her hotel room, she has felt special.

If circumstances hadn't gotten in the way, I'm sure we could have gone on to date. But that night, the universe had other plans for me. The accident certainly made me want to do things differently. Live my life in full color instead of in muted shades like I had been.

Now that I've recovered and the new book is released, it's time to gather up all those other loose ends of my life and weave them into a future.

I've got one week to make things right with Katie, and it starts this afternoon.

***

Another bookshop, and while the sights and smells are similar to this morning, this place has a whole different vibe. The shop floor is way smaller, the shelves more tightly packed, and the books less aligned, like they've been well thumbed. The books, too, are not just your run-of-the-mill high street finds and there's not a flashy coffee table book in sight. Even the readers lining up for me to sign their books are a more eclectic group.

This is the kind of bookshop that I like to explore on weekends. It takes me back to my local library, where I spent a lot of my time growing up. The dusty, dry scent of paper and cardboard was strangely comforting. I've always loved books, and if I wasn't outdoors kicking a ball around with my friends, that was where I hung out. Me, slouched in one peeling leather chair, Aaron in the one opposite, like a couple of old men rather than your typical teenage boys. Being into books meant we stayed out of trouble with the local constabulary too. We were never bored at the library, unlike our friends, who were always being rounded up and dropped home in the back of a squad car.

My smile comes more easily as, one after another, the customers place copies of my paperback on the desk in front of me. Either I'm more used to the routine now or this store is making me feel more comfortable. I think I'm actually enjoying myself. Who'd have thought it?

I look up at the twentysomething man in front of me who is saying the book is for his dad, and from the corner of my eye, I catch a glimpse of long dark hair flowing over a ruby-red coat. I know it's Katie before she even turns fully in my direction. It's the way she holds her slim shoulders, the way her long, elegant fingers comb through those glossy dark locks. A waft of her fresh, sweet perfume is carried to me on the puff of cool air that snuck through the open door behind her. It teases me into action.

"Sorry, could you repeat that name again?" I completely missed the name I need to write on the book, too distracted by Katie's arrival. I quickly finish signing the book and hand it back to the guy. Then, before the next person steps forward, I excuse myself, saying I just need to stretch my legs for a minute.

It's not a complete lie, as my right leg does lock up when I sit for long periods of time. I duck behind the sign with a giant-size closeup of my face on it. I'd rather have had a giant cover of my book than be confronted by my face everywhere, but apparently, my face will sell more books according to Jackie. At this point, I don't care what's on the signage as long as it gives me some degree of privacy as I come face to face with Katie for the first time since Christmas.

"Katie?"

"Drew …" My name is released from her lips on a whimper, but it's the almost imperceptible shake of her head that has me dropping my hand back to my sides.

She clears her throat, then in her boss lady voice asks, "How is the signing going?"

"Good, I think … Don't tell Jackie, but I'm kind of enjoying myself."

She smiles. "Who'd have thought the moody Scotsman would enjoy meeting his fans?"

"Settle down. I'm not moody," I grumble but continue to grin down at her.

She laughs, and when her head tilts back to look at me, her eyes are sparkling as bright as the stars on a clear night over the ocean in Cornwall. I can't resist the temptation to reach up with my thumb to gently touch the corner of her perfect pout. She stills instantly, the blinking of her eyes the only movement. I want to kiss those lips again, but I'm conscious of the fact that we're here in a bookshop with her staff nearby, so I do nothing more.

She presses her lips together, then says softly, "You should get back to those adoring fans of yours."

I nod, and when she goes to walk past me, I encircle her wrist with my palm before bending to whisper in her ear, "I've missed you." It's a spur-of-the-moment thing, and I can't help noticing the way she shivers slightly at my words.

I feel lighter on the walk back to my chair to complete the signings. With Katie at my side this time.

TWENTY

Katie

Seconds is all it took for me to melt under Drew's touch again. I'm so pathetic. And now I have to sit next to him, pretending I can do his version of friendship and it won't rip my heart out every time he leaves to return to his life as a hermit.

What's killing me more is the way he charms every female who steps up to get her book signed. I don't know why he had such a big issue with doing this, because he's a natural.

I slip my phone out of my bag and send a message to my group chat with Sarah, Allie, and Dana.

Me: *Help, girls. I've been here a hot minute, and already I want to do dirty things with Drew.*

The girls are the best, but lately, I suspect I've put our friendship to the test. My texting in the lead up to my first face-to-face with Drew has become a bit obsessive and probably damn annoying. I know I'd be frustrated by me. My concern about seeing Drew again has been out of control. It's been hard to concentrate on anything else. I've worried about everything from how we will greet each other all the way through to whether we'll end up having sex again. I still haven't landed on the answer to that million-dollar question.

The girls' responses ping on my phone, one after the other. I don't dare look at them with Drew sitting only feet from me. I stand up and tap Drew on his arm. "Just have to take a call with the office." I wave my phone in his face like it will add substance to my story, then walk away quickly, knowing instinctively that he is watching every step.

When I've found a relatively private corner in the bookshop, I pull out my phone again and scroll through the replies.

Sarah: *Do it.*

Allie: *What Sarah said, but only if you won't end up hurt.*

Dana: *Sometimes it's best to walk away.*

Their advice is wildly different, and I take a moment to consider each suggestion. Sarah's response is the least surprising. She's always been a free spirit, flitting from one relationship to the next, never becoming too attached. Dana's response hints at a hurt in her past that she's never felt able to share with us. Allie and I suspect she had her heart broken badly in college, because she never talks about dating. It's Allie's response that gives me pause. Drew does have the ability to hurt me. I don't believe he would do it deliberately though. He's not mean or unfeeling. But because I like him, a lot, he could unknowingly break my heart if I let him.

I turn to face out the glass window of the bookshop and come face-to-face with a life-size poster of the man himself. He's impossibly good looking. No wonder the women waiting for him to sign their books are swooning. I remember seeing this photo for the first time when Jackie showed me the proofs for all the promotional material. It made my lady bits tingle with the memory of his naked body.

This time, my reaction is different. I know him better, and those stormy gray eyes in the picture are less of a mystery. The text messaging between us over the last couple of weeks has given me more of an insight into the man. He's shared snippets of experiences, thoughts, and daily happenings in his life. Before, he was like a nice sketch, interesting and pleasing to look at. Now he's becoming an oil painting, with all the details, background, and light and dark shadings added.

Maybe it's time I discovered why he doesn't seem to want to let me go, like he told me he wanted in Cornwall. His words back then are a contradiction to his actions now. First, demanding I do the book tour, then showing up at the gala, and all the texts between us since.

I should just come straight out and ask him to explain himself, because I need to know before I fall back into his arms again. Something that is bound to happen now that I'm back in Drew's orbit. The physical attraction is impossible for me to resist. I never saw myself as weak willed, but obviously I am.

Until I'm ready to hear his reasons, though, avoidance is the only answer. Now that is something I can control, because I have my own car and will be able to travel to the next city separately from Drew.

***

At our hotel for the night, I excuse myself from Drew and Jackie, telling them I'll order room service because I have some work to do. It's true—I do have work to do. For weeks, I've avoided reading Drew's book, but I can't anymore. I pick up the copy he sent me by courier the day after release, which was sitting on the top of my overnight bag.

I've had the manuscript in my email folder for weeks, but it remains unopened. Any excuse I could come up with to not open the attachment worked for me. It was like I was back in college, needing to study for an exam but doing everything except opening the textbooks.

I put my copy of Drew's book down on the nearby table and go to get myself a glass of red wine from the minibar. But halfway across the room, I stop myself. It's just another excuse to delay the moment.

I turn back to the table and pick up the thick hardcover volume again. Every night since I received the copy from Drew, I've looked at it, sitting on the set of drawers beside my bed. Opening the book has now taken on more significance than I should have ever let happen. It's just a damn book. I've read hundreds of them, so this one doesn't need to be anything more than any other. But it's his, a part of him.

Before I knew who Drew was, I read his first book about his time in Iraq. It was heart-wrenchingly raw. Now that I know the man behind the stories, I don't know if I can bear to read it. Of course, I have to, in case I'm asked any questions as the head of Carlson Publishing.

I've delayed long enough. All my work emails are up to date, and I've completed my usual bedtime ritual, even adding an additional moisturizing body rub with the aromatherapy oils provided by the hotel. There's nothing more to do other than to climb into the cozy-looking bed and read. With the book tightly clasped in my hand, I walk over to the bed and flop down on top of it.

Hours later, tears stream down my cheeks. I've just read how one of Drew's SAS teammates was killed by a sniper on a mission in Kandahar Province, Afghanistan. He was standing right beside him. *One bullet for one life. It was destined to be mine or his,* he writes. The way he talks about his friend and his experience of loss is heartbreaking. I remember back to the way he talked about the minicab driver who died in the car accident. At the time, I wondered why he was so impacted by his death when he hadn't really known him.

Now it makes more sense. Maybe it even explains why he needed to be on his own to recover from his injuries. I get up from the bed to wash my face, then settle back down to continue. There's no way I can sleep now. I need to read another chapter. I want to learn more.

TWENTY-ONE

Katie

By day two of the book tour, I'm exhausted, and it's not even lunchtime. I sip on my second cup of coffee for the morning, hoping it will give me the energy to keep my tired body awake. It's my own fault because I was up until the early hours of the morning reading Drew's book. I didn't finish it, but only because my eyes kept drooping shut and the words were blurring together from tiredness or tears. It was hard to know which.

What I do know is that I've learned so much more about what makes Drew tick. His writing is honest, unfiltered, and intense. He shares everything—thoughts, feelings, and emotions—in some of the most horrific of circumstances. And it changes everything. How am I going to be able to look him in those stormy-gray eyes and not see the pain of loss I now know he hides from the public?

Sadly, I've also come to the conclusion that he's probably not a settling down kind of guy. In the book, he comes across as wanting his freedom to be able to find the next big adventure. After the things he's seen, it would be ridiculous to think he could possibly be content living a *regular guy* kind of life.

I skipped the Leeds bookshop this morning, for those reasons and more. However, the excuse of needing to take calls with my office or respond to emails is starting to wear thin. Even Jackie is becoming suspicious, and she knows what my workday normally entails. Avoiding being alone with Drew may have worked so far, but now I'm either going to have to spend time with him or come up with a new reason for sneaking off tomorrow.

By the time the afternoon session in York is underway, I've successfully managed to not have one minute alone with him. I'm turning into an expert at ducking and diving out of his path. I've even been able to evade his gaze and ignore his personal comments. It's all been strictly business. Not an easy thing to do when Drew's presence is so overwhelming, tempting me back to dirty thoughts.

The last of the readers eagerly await their moment with Drew, and I'm congratulating myself on surviving another day of book signings. Two down and only three to go. The privacy of my hotel room beckons. I tilt my head to Jackie, who is standing beside me. "Well done. It's been another successful day."

"Thanks, but it's not over yet. We still have dinner with the competition winners." My head spins in her direction, and I take a step back. I can tell by the way she's wringing her hands that she was worried about telling me this little piece of information. I can only imagine.

"What the hell are you talking about?" I ask shakily, trying to keep my voice low so Drew can't hear us.

Jackie offers me a small smile, and her features soften. "Drew insisted that if he was going to have dinner with a bunch of strangers, his words not mine, then we'd have to join him … I said it would be okay." Jackie stares down at the floor. "I know it might be a bit awkward, but I've met the winners, and they seem very nice." She doesn't realize the reason I'm not happy has nothing to do with having dinner with some competition winners.

She looks back up at me sheepishly. "Sorry. I should have mentioned it earlier."

I know I signed off on the concept of running a competition for fans to win a dinner with the author, but I never expected I would have to be a part of it.

"It's okay. I'm sure it will be fine," I grumble, not doing a very good job of hiding my displeasure at the idea. All my tactics to avoid Drew today have amounted to nothing now that I need to have dinner with him. And there goes my nice quiet evening finishing Drew's book.

Back at the hotel, I escape to my room almost as soon as we're through the doors, leaving Drew and Jackie discussing the details of the dinner. All I need to know is when, because Jackie told me earlier that the dinner will be in the hotel dining room.

I put a little more effort into dressing tonight than I usually would for a business dinner. I could pretend it's for the competition winners, but it's not. I want him to want me. Drew and I may not work, but it doesn't stop me from needing to know he desires me.

My outfit is not wildly inappropriate. It's just a little black dress in a classically simple wrap style. The crossover forms a deep V over my braless breasts, the band tied tightly at my waist. With my hands resting on my hips, I turn right, then left in front of the mirror, and the skirt flares out before falling loosely to mid-thigh. I like that, and with my favorite new black heels, it makes my legs look longer. I wore these shoes for the first time at the Christmas gala, and I love the way the straps bind my ankles, taking them from the ordinary to straight-out sexy with a hint of dominatrix.

I lean in closer to the mirror to do a final check of my makeup. It's subtle and light except for the smoky eyes. Allie is great at teaching me all her modeling makeup tricks and would be proud of my efforts tonight.

Soon after, I'm walking into the hotel bar to meet Drew and Jackie. I'm a few minutes late, having texted Jackie first to check that she was downstairs already. Not that it helps when two steps across the threshold, Drew has me in his crosshairs, his eyes tracking with the accuracy of a laser beam over every inch of my body. Heat floods my cheeks, and my nipples pebble with delight at his attention. Now I'm thinking the decision to go braless was a bad move, given the way the stretch fabric clings and does nothing to mask my erect nipples. My body is a traitor to his gaze.

Tiny bubbles of pleasure are bursting inside me at the look of appreciation. His eyes are a brighter blue tonight rather than gray, probably due to his pale-blue button-down shirt he's wearing with those sinfully tight black jeans. My eyes assess him as thoroughly as he does me. Why does he always have to look so hot?

I join them at the bar. "Hi, Jackie." Jackie jumps down from the stool she was sitting on. She's tiny compared to me in my killer heels.

"Hey. Wow, you look great. But I need to dash. Reception just called to say that the cars have arrived with our guests." She races toward the door, leaving us both staring after her. She explained to me earlier that they'll be arriving in the two limousines hired to pick up each winner and their invited guest. They're all local since the entry to the competition was only possible in person at the two bookshops today.

Drew clears his throat, and I turn to face him. "You look beautiful tonight," he says in his deep bedroom voice. His eyes smolder with so much heat you could toast marshmallows by them. It melts me from the inside out.

"Would you like a drink?" he asks, and I press my suddenly dry lips together. His gaze zeroes in on them. I look toward the bar, avoiding his stare and pretending that I'm trying to choose.

"Maybe just a glass of sparkling water. It's been a long day." He nods, then turns to place my order. I'm sure he was about to say something but changed his mind. I wonder what it was as we stand there silently side by side, watching the bartender pour my drink.

I don't have to wonder for long. When the drink is placed on the bar, Drew passes it to me, then asks, "Katie, why are you avoiding me?" I nearly drop the glass.

"Now isn't the time," I tell him, noticing Jackie at the door with four women standing just behind her. "Our guests are here."

He leans into me and whispers, "Later." His deep-timbral voice sends a shiver up my spine. It's not fair that every time he uses his panty-dropping bedroom voice on me, I melt into a puddle of longing.

TWENTY-TWO

Drew

There she goes again, wearing an outfit that shoots blood straight to my cock. I'm trying to work out whether she's a temptress or a tease. Prior experience would lead me to believe it's the former, not the latter. It's an intoxicating combination, an innocent blush with her sexy little body that I already know is made for sin.

I want to throw her over my shoulder, then march us right back up to my room so I can fuck her senseless. I need the release, and I suspect she does too. Tension is practically emanating from the pores of her skin, and that's how it's been since we saw each other yesterday. The last one and a half days have tested my patience and resolve to wait for a sign from her before I dive in and take what I want.

I can almost see her good angel and bad angel warring with each other. It's in the tiny, cute frown lines between her brows, the unnaturally stiff way she holds her shoulders, and the constant twisting of the ring on her right hand. I smile at the memory of her telling me it's the one her stepdad gave her for her twenty-first birthday.

We are sitting at a round table, and Katie has maneuvered the seating arrangements so she's the farthest away. I know she's been avoiding me; any idiot could see that, but the fact she can't even look me in the eye is a worrying new development. I'm not sure what it means. All I do know is I don't like it. Her expressive eyes are a portal to her thoughts and feelings, and without the opportunity to see into the dark depths, I'm lost. Tonight, there is no softening in those deep pools. They remain dark and troubled, contradicting the way her nipples instantly hardened into peaks, poking at the fabric of her dress when she saw me checking her out earlier.

I turn back to the competition winner on my right, who is still talking, and move my arm away from the lady on my left. I'm trying really hard to be polite, but if she doesn't stop stroking my arm every chance she gets, I'm going to lose my shit. Why the fuck did I agree to this? It's like I've found my way into a bad dream.

The two winners of the competition were each allowed to bring a guest. One lady brought her daughter, and the other her best friend. From the moment they walked in, squealed with excitement, and threw their arms around me upon introduction, I knew I was in trouble. Who does that when they meet someone for the first time? It's like I'm a piece of fresh meat thrown in amongst a cage of lionesses, each of them trying to get their pound of flesh.

The lady to my right raises her voice louder, vying for my attention by babbling in an overexcited, high-pitched voice about the last time she visited Scotland. Her voice becomes more trill with each glass of champagne she consumes. I look pleadingly at Katie and Jackie, hoping one of them will save me from this hellish experience.

There's only one thing for it: more alcohol to drown them out. I pick up my glass of champagne and realize it's empty. Good, I hate that shit anyway, and I need something way more fortifying. "Excuse me, ladies, but I'm going to the bar. Who wants a drink?"

"Me," Katie responds in a clipped tone almost as soon as the words have left my mouth.

"Me too," the ladies around the table chime in, then giggle like a bunch of schoolgirls, which is frankly ridiculous because three of them look to be my mother's age.

The one younger girl is the twentysomething daughter of the lady on my right, and she hasn't said one word all evening. Not that she could get a word in with her mother dominating the conversation and cutting down anyone who dares to stop her flow of pointless chatter.

"Katie, could you help me with the drinks?" I ask, and she jumps up from her seat, then quickly asks around the table, gathering the ladies' orders. Jackie offers to help, but Katie reassures her that we've got this and follows me to the bar. It looks like all of us are wanting to escape from the table.

Once Katie and I have placed the order, we turn to face each other.

"This dinner was a terrible idea, wasn't it?" she says, looking up at me. It's the first time she's truly held my gaze all day, and it's not like I haven't been trying.

I sigh. "Aye, it was," I mutter, wishing we were already done and it was just Katie and me having a drink together.

"I'll speak to the waiter on the way back to ask him to move things along quicker."

"Thanks. If I have to listen to that woman tell me one more

of her travel stories or even worse, have the other one stroke me like I'm a dog or something, I'm going—" I don't get to finish my sentence before Katie interrupts.

"Cats or dogs? Choose one."

"What?"

"I just realized I've never asked you. Do you prefer cats or dogs?"

I smile at her silly question. "Dogs, of course. Man's best friend and all that."

"I prefer dogs too," she tells me with one of her beautiful smiles directed at me and only me. And just like that, she's managed to lighten my mood.

The bartender places the last of the drinks on the bar in front of us.

"Are you ready to face another feeding frenzy?" she asks with another smile that feels like it's just for me. I guess I wasn't the only one that thought the ladies were out for meat.

I pick up my scotch whiskey. "Just a minute. I need some of this first." I take a big gulp, enjoying the burn in my throat as it slips down.

She places her hand on my arm, and the warmth of her touch does more for me than the fiery drink. "Thanks for doing this, Drew." Then, realizing where her hand is, she quickly withdraws it. "Sorry. I didn't mean to stroke you like a dog," she teases.

"You, beautiful, can stroke me anytime you want." We stare at each other for a moment. I don't know what she's thinking, but with the sparkle in her eye, I suspect it might be the same as me, and she's remembering the last time she stroked my cock.

"We should get back," she murmurs, but it's another full minute before she moves.

Within the hour, we're back at the bar, sitting on the barstools. This time, it's Jackie on my left and Katie on my right. The ladies have been sent on their way, and we've debriefed on the evening. We have agreed unanimously that there will be no more competitions.

Jackie interrupts, "Umm, I think I'll go to bed." I don't miss the look Katie directs Jackie's way or how her knuckles whiten on her hold of the glass when Jackie says by way of explanation, "I'm exhausted, and we've an early start for the drive to Edinburgh."

When Jackie is out of earshot, I lean toward Katie and whisper, "Alone at last." Her sharp intake of breath is the only indication that she has heard me. The situation is getting ridiculous. I thought that after my apology at the gala, things would be better. Okay, maybe the orgasm following the apology was too soon, but since then, we've been getting along fine through text. There should be no reason for her to avoid me now that we're finally able to see each other face-to-face.

This time on the book tour was meant to bring us together, not pull us further apart.

"I've been reading your book," Katie announces when the silence between us drags on.

I can't help asking, "And what do you think?"

With only a slight tilt of her head, she looks at me sideways. "You're a brilliant writer."

"Is that your professional or personal opinion?"

"Both. Your words are very moving," she says, her voice just a little more than a whisper.

My chest swells with pride. I wonder if she realizes how much her opinion means to me.

We sit silently, sipping on our drinks for a few more minutes.

I don't want to ruin this moment, but it may be the only chance I get to speak to her alone. I begin, "Katie, it seems to me that we need to talk."

She turns slowly on her stool to face me, like she was expecting me to say those words.

"Fine. You can start," she says before wrapping her arms around her waist.

Her defiant words are a little surprising, but I've learned to be prepared for the unexpected with Katie. "I'll go back to my earlier question. Why are you avoiding me?"

A grimace flashes across her face so briefly, I think I may have imagined it. "Okay, it's because every time I'm near you, I lose all sense of what's right."

"What do you think is right, Katie? Because I suspect we have very different ideas."

"What's right? I'm not sure, but I do know what's wrong. Every time I'm with you, I end up falling back into your arms. I feel like I lose myself in you."

"See, I would have said that's right. Our chemistry is explosive and impossible to ignore." She frowns. Little creases are etched between her brows, and the corners of her mouth are drawn down. My thumb itches to smooth the lines, and I want to kiss a smile back onto her lips.

"Fine, I agree that the sexual chemistry between us is unique. But the fact is, I don't do casual flings. Our one-night stand was my first and last. I'm just not able to separate the sex from my feelings. I need a relationship, and you don't want one."

"You don't know what I want," I respond, and the words come out more harshly than I mean to. The truth is, I don't know what I want. What am I doing here with Katie? Am I just looking for something casual like she accuses, or do I want more?

Her head lowers. "No, I guess I don't. Isn't that the problem though?" she mumbles. Then she lifts her eyes back to mine. She stares at me like she's waiting for me to say more. I don't know what to say, and each second I let the cold silence continue, the spark in her eyes is slowly extinguished.

"Look, we're not going to resolve anything tonight. As Jackie said, we have an early start tomorrow. I'm going to bed." She touches me briefly on my arm, and what seconds ago felt like ice in my veins heats up again. "Good night, Drew."

She leaves, and I lean my elbows on the bar. The bartender moves closer and asks if I want another. I nod, and when he places the tumbler of whiskey in front of me, I throw it back, gesturing for one more.

I know the answer to what I want is not at the bottom of a whiskey glass, but it sure as hell feels better thinking about it when you're steaming drunk.

The refill arrives, and I sip on this one slowly. Through the alcoholic buzz, I replay my conversation with Katie. I've never been in a proper relationship, but it's not like it was a deliberate decision. It was more the life I was leading meant I was never in one place long enough. The question is, could I commit now with Katie?

Maybe.

One thing I do know is I need to be sure before my next move, because I never want to hurt her.

TWENTY-THREE

Katie

We're in the beautiful city of Edinburgh, and this afternoon's book signing is in another independent bookshop. The difference with this one is the view from the front door up the cobbled street to Edinburgh Castle. I've already come outside twice to see it since we arrived nearly two hours ago. I don't think I'll ever get over the excitement of seeing real castles. It's probably a carryover from my childhood when I loved dressing up as a princess.

I step back inside and walk over to join Jackie. Drew glances up and smiles when he sees me. He's done the same thing each time I've come back in. I thought things would be a little awkward after our brief but intense chat last night. But it hasn't been the case at all.

I'm confused because of the way we left things. Finally telling him I'm looking for a relationship felt good. It was his lack of response that kept me up half the night. If I'm ever going to get another good night's sleep, we need to finish the conversation. But not till after the interview tomorrow. I know he's worried about it, and I don't want to make things worse by confronting him over the question of us.

With his head down laughing while he signs a book, Drew looks tired but happier today than he's been at any other stop. I'm guessing it's because his family will be coming by later. They live not far from the city, and it's kind of sweet that he wants them to be part of his success. I like that he has strong family ties, especially after his tough early years with his father.

The clock on the far wall tells me his family should be arriving in about fifteen minutes. I lean toward Jackie and say, "We might need to wrap things up here. Drew's mother should be arriving soon." The line is still about twenty people long. Today, like every other day, we've run over due to the number of people showing up to have their books signed. The popularity of the signings is being reflected in the sales numbers and ranking of Drew's book. I checked late last night, and his book is edging closer to the number one spot for paperbacks on the UK bestsellers list. One more day, and we may have something big to celebrate.

Shortly after, Drew signs the last book, stands, then stretches his arms wide before walking slowly toward me. His limp is more noticeable when he sits for long periods of time.

He stops next to me and rubs his thigh, and I have to ask, "How's the leg?" I know how much he hates anyone asking, but I'm feeling guilty for leaving him sitting for nearly two hours without a break.

He frowns. "I've had better days. But it's my own fault. I might have had one too many whiskeys last night and fallen over my bag in my room."

"What? Really? You seemed fine when I left you in the bar."

He shakes his head. "That was the problem. Being dumped by a beautiful woman. I had to drown my sorrows or deal with a case of blue balls." His grin when he looks back up is cheeky and sexy all rolled into one. I'm sure my heart skips a beat before racing on.

We only have two more days, then this smooth-talking temptation can go back to Cornwall, and my heart will be safe again, I tell myself. He's much easier to handle when we're texting.

I'm still working on a verbal response when a squat older woman comes out of nowhere, and like a heat-seeking missile, barrels straight into Drew's body. With an *oof* that turns into a laugh, Drew wraps his arms tightly around the woman who barely reaches his shoulder height. This must be his mother.

She steps back a little, but keeping her arms around him, she says, "Andrew, ye look like something the cat dragged in." Her voice is stern, even though her grin is as broad as her son's. I hide a smile behind my hand. Mothers always know when you're hungover.

"And it's good to see you too, Mum," he jokes before they release each other.

A guy with almost the same blue-gray eyes as Drew steps forward, and they hug. "How's it going?" the guy asks Drew, and he just grins back at him. This has to be his brother. It's not possible that two people could have the same unusually colored eyes and not be related.

Drew turns back to me, grinning. "Katie, I'd like you to meet my mother, Aileen, and my brother, Rory. Mum, Rory, this is my boss, Katie." I scowl at him for his use of the word boss, but he knows I don't mean it.

His mom takes my hand. "Aye, right! I cannot believe this wee bonnie lass is ye boss." My eyes widen. If I thought Drew was hard to understand sometimes, I have no hope of understanding his mother's stronger accent.

Drew seems to notice my confusion and leans down to me. "It

means she likes you."

I blush, and his mom swats him on the arm. "I feel sorry for yer, having to deal with this un. He can be an eijit. Maybe you can knock some sense into him." I smile. I've heard people use the word eijit before, so I know she means idiot. I imagine Drew has done some crazy things in his time that would give his mom sleepless nights.

Drew squirms and quickly turns to introduce Jackie before he walks his mother over to the table with a stack of his books on it. He's beaming as he takes two copies of the book from the pile, signs them, and hands one to his mother and one to his brother. This is a softer side of Drew I've never seen before, and it makes my heart ache to know that in a few days this special man will walk away from me again. I turn and walk back outside to look one more time at the castle.

Minutes later, Drew joins me. "Why do you keep disappearing on me?"

I point up the road to the glimpse of the castle wall. "Edinburgh Castle is beautiful. I guess you don't notice it so much having grown up near here, but to an American like me, it's pretty amazing."

He smiles. "Aye, it is … Ah, I was wondering … would you like to join my family and me for dinner tonight?"

I do a double take. "You're *asking* me to join you?" This has got to be the first time he has asked rather than demanded. He's making it so hard for me to put some distance between us.

He looks down at me with his head tipped to the side. "Katie, I wouldn't ask if I didn't want you to come … And it will just be at the hotel. With the interview tomorrow, it won't be a late night." He says the word interview like it leaves a nasty taste in his mouth. I know he hates the idea of the interview, which is why he wanted his family—and me, for some reason—to be here for this part of the tour. It was one of his nonnegotiable conditions, according to Jackie.

"Okay. Maybe you need someone to make sure there's no more

late-night drinking."

He chuckles. "That's never going to work when you're the reason for my late-night drinking."

That's the second time today he's insinuated that he got drunk last night because of me.

***

We arrived at the studio just before dawn this morning, and immediately, Drew was rushed off down a corridor to makeup. Jackie ushered his mother and brother toward a table that had been set up with coffee and tea facilities while I just stood and watched all the activity around me. I haven't had a coffee yet myself, because honestly, I don't think I could keep it down. Today, the butterflies are not only fluttering in my stomach, but they're doing a full acrobatic routine that would earn them a ten at the Olympics. I can only imagine how Drew is feeling.

"Are we all set?" I ask Jackie when she comes to stand beside me. She's just returned with Drew, who is now over talking to the producer.

To the people gathered around him, he probably seems cool and calm, but I can tell he's nervous. The smile he's giving the producer is strained, and he keeps looking over at the door like he expects someone to come through it any minute. I know how much he hates being the center of attention and being in the public eye. Even having all these people fussing over him can't be easy.

The producer walks away, and I wander over to the small group who he is standing with. "Drew, can I have a word?" He nods sharply. "Please excuse us for just a moment," I tell the group, then take his elbow and lead him away to a quieter corner.

"Are you okay?"

"I'm either going to freeze or puke my guts up. I'm just fucking glad there's no live audience." I reach my hand up and place it on the cool crisp cotton of his shirt in the region of his heart. It's racing.

We look deep into each other's eyes.

"You've got this," I tell him when someone announces five minutes.

"Kiss me," he demands gruffly.

Without even thinking, I stretch up, and he bends down. Our lips come together in a kiss full of emotion and heat. My hand still resting on his chest feels the beats steady as the kiss lengthens. He breaks the connection first.

"Good luck," I whisper. He nods, then turns and walks over to the producer.

I follow to take my seat between his mom and Jackie.

"All right, hen?" his mom asks as she reaches for my hand. "Ye shakin' like a leaf, lass." I look down at our clasped hands. Her old, work-worn one covering my younger one. It reminds me of my own mother and how she has always comforted me when I've been worried.

"I'm worried for him. I know how much he hates doing this kind of thing."

She nods. "Aye! But ye have to let 'em fly. My Andrew has always flown close to the sun. One day, when ye have bairns of your own, you'll understand." I'm not sure I'm following what she means about having children of my own one day, other than that she tries not to worry about Drew following his dreams. Either way, her tone and the squeeze of the hand are reassuring.

The interview starts slow with a simple recap of where he grew up and his SAS training. His answers are clear, with a sprinkling of humor. He talks about his time in Iraq and Afghanistan, which is the basis of the book. The audience is going to love him.

Then, just as the interview is coming to an end, the host asks, "Now, all the women out there are dying to know—is there a special someone in your life?" They aren't supposed to ask him questions about his personal life. The questions should all be about the book.

He laughs congenially, then replies almost immediately, "Aye, but she's a very private person."

What? Does he mean me or someone else? I'd hardly consider myself as someone special to him. He couldn't even tell me last night what he wants from us. Besides all that, I'm not exactly a private person when I've lived most of my life in the public spotlight. It can't be me.

It tears me apart to think there may be someone else from his past, and as the interview winds down, I excuse myself from his mother, saying I need to make a work call.

I walk outside and suck in some much-needed fresh air. We've got no other events today and don't leave for Birmingham until late tomorrow. I only need to hold it together till I'm back in the privacy of my room.

TWENTY-FOUR

Drew

What's up with Katie? Back at the hotel after the interview, she couldn't escape to her room fast enough. I didn't follow her because I'd promised my mom that we would have lunch together before she and Rory went home. I was going to invite Katie to come with us, but she disappeared before I could even get the words out.

Lunch was booked at a fancy restaurant in the center of the city, and it lived up to every one of the excellent reviews I read online. It was the kind of place I never imagined I would be able to afford. It feels good being able to treat my mom and brother in this way.

Mom and I stand side by side outside the restaurant, waiting for

Rory. He's gone to get the car from the nearby parking garage.

"Ye know, my lad, I'm very proud of what ye've done," Mom says, continuing to look up the street rather than at me. I've always known she was proud of all of her children, but I think this might be the first time she's said it to me.

I put my arm around her slim shoulders and hug her into my side. "Aye, Mum. I know."

Surprisingly, instead of hugging me back, she nudges me in the ribs. "Katie is a bonnie lass." I'm amazed she's waited this long to bring up the subject of Katie. I saw them sitting together during the interview, and they looked to be getting along really well. Just like I knew they would.

"Aye, Mum, I have noticed how beautiful she is."

"Yer off yer head if yer don't do something about her. I like her." I smile. I certainly would be mad to not try to make things work between Katie and me.

"I'm working on it, Mum."

She smiles at me, and this time when she leans in, I get a hug, not a jab. Rory pulls the car up to the curb, and I open the door for my mother. When she's settled, Rory leans across and asks, "You sure you don't want a ride back to the hotel?"

"Aye. The short walk will be good exercise for my leg," I tell him, and he nods. Then with a final farewell, they drive off.

The truth is, I wanted the fresh air to clear my head before I go see Katie. It's time we finished our conversation from last night. Mom is right. I need to stop stuffing around and do something to show Katie that she means more to me than just a good time. We've established our sexual chemistry is real, and now I need to prove that my feelings go deeper. It's not going to be easy when, up until now, I've been eluding her. The first night, I snuck out of her hotel room, then in Cornwall, I sent her away. And even in New York, I left her in the dark meeting room. I've told her I want her, but I've never shown it.

I've been such a fucking idiot. It's time I let her know in words and actions that I want to be with her.

***

Number thirty-six. Katie's room at the hotel. It's not hard to find since it's right beside mine. I lift my hand and knock three times. She said she had work to do, so I'm assuming she's in there. Although by the way she raced off earlier, anything is possible.

This morning before the interview, when I kissed her, it felt like the planets had finally aligned for us. I thought we were good. But by the end of the interview, her mood had shifted. I wish I knew what had changed. Then I'd be better prepared for this chat.

I rub my leg, impatiently waiting for her to open the door. And when she's standing before me, all my prepared words fly out of my head. She's gorgeous, as always, with her hair pulled back tightly into a ponytail and dressed casually in a tank top and leggings.

I step forward, not waiting to be invited in, even though I should. I guess it's okay, because she steps back to let me pass. When the door is closed behind us, I turn and pull her into my arms. She doesn't resist. I want to recapture the feeling of our kiss from this morning, but one look into her eyes tells me that she doesn't want my kisses.

"Why did you run away so quickly after the interview?" I ask. It's not what I planned to say, but it comes out anyway. I need to understand what's going on behind her sad eyes.

She pulls back, and I instantly drop my arms. It feels like we've been here before.

"Drew, I can't do this again without knowing … Has there been anyone else?" My mouth drops open. Of all the things I thought she was going to say, that wasn't one of them.

With a finger under her chin, I lift her face to mine. "Katie, there has been no one else since our one-night stand. There could be no one but you. Don't you understand? I want *you*."

She stands statue still in front of me, her only movement the rapid blinking of her dark eyes as she searches mine.

I reach out to take her hands in mine. "Last night when I didn't speak up, it's because I hadn't really thought much further ahead than us seeing each other. You made me stop and consider what comes next. I want to take you to dinner, then on other dates. See how things go … Whatever you want for us, I want it too."

Katie breathes deeply as she continues to stare at me. I wish she would say something, because for once I can't read what's behind her tear-filled eyes. Are they good tears or bad tears?

"Kiss me," she whispers finally, and I think I must have imagined it until she repeats it louder. "Kiss me."

I bend my head and seal my lips to hers. The kiss is like the one from this morning. Full of emotion and heat. But there is also something else. A deeper something that I want to cling to tightly and never let go of. I lift one hand to cup her head, holding her closer.

The connection of this moment feels bigger than just the touch of her lips to mine or the dueling of our tongues. She's become the air I breathe, and I ache for more.

Slowly, I begin to trail kisses from her mouth to her jawline, then to that sensitive spot below her ear and down her neck. Her head tilts to one side so I can run the kisses down to her collarbone. I want to cover every inch of her body with my mouth. The soft, sweet sounds slipping from her lips give me all the encouragement I need.

Her fingers grasp at the hem of my T-shirt, and I stop for a moment to tug it off.

I want her hands on me.

I want her painted nails digging into my skin as she screams out her release.

Katie pulls her tank top off over her head, and her bare breasts bounce free, no longer hidden from me. I reach out to cup her tits in my palms, and she lays her hands on my shoulders. The feel of her warm, soft skin just makes me want more.

"I want you naked."

"And I want you naked," she replies with a sexy smile.

It's been too long since we were last completely alone, free to explore each other's body without the threat of interruption.

We strip out of our remaining clothes. Leggings, jeans, boxers, and silky panties thrown aside. When there is nothing between us, we fall into each other feverishly. Skin against skin. I move her backward till the backs of her knees hit the bed base, and she tumbles onto the firm mattress, spread out before me like the most lavish feast.

"Beautiful." Her folds are already glistening under the neatly trimmed landing strip of dark hair.

I kneel on the floor at the foot of the bed and pull her toward me. With one hand on each of her thighs, I gently ease them apart, then bury my face between her legs, nuzzling in close and swiping my tongue through the slickness just once from back to front, deliberately not reaching her clit. She tastes amazing.

"Damn you," she mutters, and her hips wriggle, trying to push me closer. I know what she wants, but I want her to tell me.

"If there's something you want me to do, you'll need to say it." I want to hear her talk dirty to me.

"Grr … suck my pussy." Her husky, desperate tone has my dick twitching to fill her, but not yet. Instead, I push my tongue into her channel as far as I can, devouring her. Her hips writhe beneath me, lifting off the bed.

Time to turn up the heat further. Holding open her folds with my thumbs, I run my tongue along them all the way to her clit. Her thighs clamp firmly around my head. I know she's close, so I sink two fingers deep into her channel.

She rocks her hips, fucking my fingers, so I add another. The passion builds; I bury my mouth between her legs again. This time, alternating between tongue flicks and gently sucking on her clit. Katie's moans reach a crescendo. Her hands clutch at my head, her nails scraping through my short hair when I seal my lips to her nub. She likes that best.

Almost instantly, she's crying out her release, her head thrashing side to side on the bed. Her body clenches tight on my fingers, not easing up until her breathing slows. I remove my fingers and one by one lick them clean, then slowly run my tongue along her folds one more time. Delicious.

"That was … sooo … good," she gasps, opening her eyes and smiling at me like she's just won the lottery. What she doesn't realize is that we've only just started.

"Only good? I'll have to try harder since I was aiming for at least mind-blowing." I swipe my hand across my mouth, then crawl up her body to drop a quick kiss to her lips. "Now the fun times begin."

Pulling up to standing, I pick her up and flip her over. Delighted squeals fill the air.

"You liked that, I gather," I say, unable to hold back my own laughter. "Now get on your knees for me, baby."

She does as I ask, and my cock twitches in anticipation. I grab a couple of pillows from the bed and prop them under her hips.

"Spread your legs," I demand, then more gently I say, "I want to see how much your body wants me."

I'm trying hard to rein in the sexual control. I know Katie would be happy to comply with my demands, but tonight isn't about that. This has to be about giving and taking equally.

"Are you ready for me to make you scream my name?"

"You talk a big game, mister … Let's see if you can rock my

world," she says, looking over her shoulder at me. Her eagerness is a huge turn-on. I line up my cock with her entrance.

"Hold on tight, baby. This is going to be a wild ride." And with no further delay, I begin to ease into her warm, welcoming body. Slowly, inch by inch, her channel adjusts until I'm balls deep.

"Are you okay?" She feels so fucking good squeezing tightly around my shaft. But I need her to tell me she's enjoying this too.

"Amazing. I feel so full." She pushes back into me. "But I need wild … not gentle and slow."

"Aye. That I can deliver." I don't need to be asked twice.

Withdrawing nearly completely, I dive back in, her walls squeezing tighter around me as she builds to another release. The question is whether I'll be able to hold on. My eyes are already rolling back into my head with the restraint to not blow my load too soon.

Katie throws her head back, her ponytail brushing against my hand. It's impossible to resist. With a few twists, the dark silky strands are wrapped around my fist. I give a gentle tug, and her hips push back in jerky movements. She's a greedy little thing when she wants her release. I pump into her harder and faster, reaching around her body to put pressure on her clit. One touch of her sensitive nub is all it takes, and her walls are spasming around me with her second orgasm.

This time, I'm with her for the whole explosive release. I come long and hard as her body milks me dry before I finally collapse over her, my upper body to her back as I curl close, my arm around her waist supporting both of us.

"Hey, are you okay?" I murmur next to her ear.

Her response is muffled in the pillow. "I think so."

"Well, let's get you cleaned up, then." I withdraw slowly, then jump up.

Katie's head turns to the side to look at me, her cheek still pushed into the pillow. "Do I really have to move?"

I chuckle. "Aye, I've made you very messy. If you sit up, I can do the rest."

She drags herself to sitting, and I bend to lift her.

"Wait! Is your leg okay to take my weight?" she asks, and it doesn't bother me. I've come a long way in accepting and acknowledging my limitations. Though this is not one of them.

"My legs are much stronger. Besides, you weigh hardly anything."

Her arms come around my neck, and her head rests against my chest. This is where she belongs.

I carry her into the spacious bathroom and deposit her next to the large built-in bathtub, then turn on the water, adjusting the temperature until it runs warm. The extra cost for this hotel was worth it just for the great water pressure and abundance of hot water. Not always guaranteed at cheaper hotels.

I turn back to Katie. "Now let's see if I can wash you properly. Our last one in Cornwall was a half-assed attempt because of my legs."

She smiles at me. "I remember your half-assed attempt as being pretty special."

When the tub is half filled and I've added enough shower gel to coat the water with a layer of foamy bubbles, I take her hand and help her in.

I slide into the tub behind her, one leg on either side of her body. "Lean back against me. I think you'll find this is going to be so much better than a shower."

TWENTY-FIVE

Katie

I rub my hand across my forehead to ease the ache that's been building since I came out of the bathtub. At some point over the last hour, while I lay back against Drew's solid chest and he lathered the soap gently over my body, I realized I never wanted this to end.

I've fallen in love with him … and I don't know what that means for us.

I don't want just the memories of the man to keep me warm at night. I want the man himself. I want to feel his arms around me when I fall asleep and again when I wake up in the morning.

I know he said, *Whatever you want for us, I want it too,* but he doesn't understand that now I want everything.

He talked of dinner dates and seeing how things go, which doesn't sound like the *happily ever after* I'm looking for with the man I love. I bury my face in my hands. Why can't I be more like Sarah and just be happy with a bunch of special moments? Instead, I have to fall for the guy who is continually reminding me that we've got great chemistry. I don't disagree, I just need more.

Drew has gone to his room to change for dinner, and I'm supposed to be doing the same. Instead, my head is spinning with all my second-guessing and ridiculous hypotheticals. I continue to pace the length of the room, my arms wrapping the bathrobe tightly around me. It's ten steps each way, and I have no idea why I counted the distance other than it might help to distract me somehow.

I need to tell him I love him. I stop. *No, it's too soon.*

I continue my pacing. I need to leave. *No, I can't run away from this; we need to talk.*

The conversations in my head go back and forth and come to one conclusion. He doesn't want what I want. I live a high-profile lifestyle in the city. And he wants to live quietly on a remote headland. It's impossible. Even if he wants to try, in the end, he'll just decide to leave again.

I need to protect my heart before he can shatter it into so many pieces I won't be able to put it back together.

I'm completely overwhelmed by the pure insanity of the thoughts flooding my brain. I start throwing some of my clothes into my bag, but I'm stopped in my tracks at the sound of Drew's knock on my door.

I have to be the logical one here and tell him we're done. It's the only option to save us from more heartache. I take a deep breath and pull the door open. It bangs back against the wall.

Drew's gray eyes instantly turn from smiling to wide open. "Hey, what's going on? Why aren't you dressed?"

I turn and walk away, putting distance between us. I don't think

I can say what I need to say while looking at him.

I keep my back to him, but I know he followed me into the room. His cologne swirls in the breeze from the air conditioner behind him. I wish he didn't always smell and look so good.

"Katie, why have you packed your bag when we're here for another night?" he asks, his voice flat, nothing like it was only a short time ago.

I look down at the shirt in my hand. How did I get here? How did I turn into a crazy person just because I've realized I'm in love? The frenetic energy of the last few minutes seeps from my body.

I turn and look up at him. "I think I have to go."

He comes a step closer, his arms stretching around me, and I weakly lean into him. I don't look up; my emotions are too turbulent and raw. I don't want him to see everything in my eyes. I don't want him to know how fragile I feel.

"Tell me what's wrong."

"I can't do this anymore. It hurts too much when you leave." My eyes sting with unshed tears.

"Katie, I'm not leaving. Will you please look at me?"

I shake my head. "But you will after one night or two. Each time, it gets harder."

"No, baby, not this time. I'm not leaving you. If you want me to stay, I'll stay. I thought you knew that. I should have been clearer. What is happening between us is so much more than sex," he promises, and I want so badly to believe his words.

Out of nowhere, I blurt out, "I love you." I don't mean the words to escape my heart, but now that they have, a knot of tension eases in my chest. I know this may not be what he wants to hear, but it feels good to say it. I've told him exactly how I feel, and now it's his turn.

"Katie, look at me," he begs, and this time I can't resist his pleading tone. My eyes slowly rise to meet his.

"Good girl." He places his finger under my chin, and when he holds my gaze, he says, "I'm not leaving, Katie, because I love you too. I want to be with you more than I've ever wanted anyone. I love you. Please let me prove it to you." The tears I've been holding back slip silently down my cheeks in a mascara-laden messy streak.

"Please don't cry. It breaks me," he whispers into my hair before he gently wipes the tears away with his thumb. When he's done, he eases my head to rest against his shoulder. I can hear the pounding of his heart beneath my ear. It's racing.

"How?" I mumble, and the word gets lost somewhere in the kiss I place in the center of his ribcage.

"What was that?" he murmurs, his chin resting on my head.

I lift my head slightly to look up at him. "How will you prove it to me?"

His chest rises with a deep breath, then falls beneath me. "Okay. For a start, I will do promotions for the book in the States, but only if you do it with me. Every book signing together. Every night after the signing together. Then I will base myself in London the majority of the time and only go remote when I'm writing."

I squeeze him tighter to me. "You would do that for me?" My voice is soft and weak.

"Aye, my bonnie lass. I would do that and so much more."

My heart is leaping in my chest. "I think you've got a deal." Everything he just said has silenced my doubts so successfully. I believe him. And he loves me.

He grins. "Let's seal the deal. And after, we can order room service. We can have our first dinner date another night." He releases one arm from me, using it to shove my bag sitting at the end of the bed onto the floor. Then, picking me up, he throws me onto the cleared bedspread.

Between giggles, I ask, "Tell me again that you love me." It's amazing that three little words can change everything.

He leans down to untie the belt on my bathrobe and pull the

edges of the fabric apart. I'm naked again. He quickly undresses too.

His gray eyes darken as he looks down at me. "I love you, Katie," he tells me over and over again, and each time is punctuated with a kiss on various parts of my body.

My heart fills a little more with love for this special man.

***

Yawning, I stretch my arms wide and hit a solid wall of muscle. My eyes spring open, and I blink several times, a smile spreading across my mouth so wide my cheeks ache. He's still here.

This has been our first whole night together. I wouldn't mind waking up every morning to the sight of Drew lying beside me on his back, buck naked except for the white sheet tented across his hips.

Drew's lean, muscled body has the unique ability to turn me into a simpering, needy, hot mess. A bit like I am now.

I look across the room at the clothes strewn on the floor from the bag I half packed yesterday in a panic. Normally, I'm a very neat person, but today, I don't care. I'm in love. And I can think of love without having a complete freak-out.

Today, I can even say that to Drew, and he will probably say the same back to me.

Beside me, the sexy man who loves me lifts one arm, dropping it across his head and displaying his sculpted triceps. My fingers itch to dive into the warm flesh or climb in underneath and snuggle. I can't resist, and just like I've dipped a spoon into a tub of Ben & Jerry's, I lean over and lick.

A groan of pleasure rumbles from the body my tongue is loving on. I smile into the warm skin of his side.

"Good morning," I murmur before turning the licks into soft, fluttery kisses. He wriggles and releases a laugh that borders on a giggle.

I lift up onto my elbow and grin down at him. "Mr. Campbell …

are you ticklish, by any chance?"

He peeks at me with one eye, his arm still bent over the other one. "Maybe?" he admits in a low voice. He sounds nervous. I run my hand gently over the area I was just kissing.

I laugh. "Really? The big, tough SAS dude turned author is ticklish? I love that you have a regular weakness, an Achilles' heel."

He moves to turn onto his side to face me, and the sheet slips from his hips, giving me a full view of his naked body. Everywhere is hard, delicious muscle. And I mean everywhere.

"Aye, I'm a regular guy with weaknesses." He nuzzles into my neck for a kiss, and my shoulder hitches with the shot of pleasure it triggers through my body. He lifts his head and grins at me. "Have I mentioned I have another weakness? You."

I roll my eyes. "And it seems a weakness for cheesy lines," I joke.

"Come on, you love my cheesy lines. I can tell. You get goose bumps on your arms and your nipples." He trails a finger up my arm and across my shoulders before going lower to brush across one pebbled nipple, then the other. He owns my body's reaction to his touch.

"I like how responsive you are to me," he says, almost like he could read my thoughts.

I return to stroking his body, my hand moving lower until I trail my index finger along the length of his shaft.

His cock visibly thickens. "Now who's responsive to touch?"

"Aye, my love. I prefer your hand on my cock to mine. It's been a long six months of jerking off in the shower."

"Poor you. But it was the same for me. I've only had my magic wand for company. It's not the same as your hand or tongue."

The hand slowly stroking across my breasts stops. "What is a magic wand?"

I can feel my cheeks heating up under his penetrating gaze. "My vibrator."

"All right. Did you think about me when you were getting off?"

I nod. I can't say the words as my face is already flooded with embarrassment. I've never thought I was shy about sex, but then I've never talked to a guy about using my vibrator. I'm uncomfortable but Drew obviously isn't. He looks like he wants to ask more, so I distract him by encircling his cock completely in my hand and pumping up and down.

It works. His hand moves to my body. There is no more speaking, just a lot of doing over the next hour.

***

Later, when we're showered and dressed for the day, we grab coffee to go from a nearby café and wander in the direction of the castle. It's a little chilly today, but I barely notice with my hand tucked into the crook of Drew's elbow. It's kind of romantic, and that alone is enough to warm me from the inside out.

"Will you tell me more about yourself?" Drew asks, and I'm surprised by the question.

I turn my head, wanting to see his face, wondering where this is going. "What would you like to know?"

I had thought we'd covered families and friends. Maybe it feels different now and he wants more.

"I don't know. Maybe something that I can't find by Googling Katie Carlson. Something you would only share with those closest to you."

My heart pounds to the beat of one of those slow love songs you hear at the end of a Hallmark movie.

I tuck in closer to his body. His question reminds me of the day we ate lunch on his deck in Cornwall and he asked about my family. But this time, it feels different. It's me he wants to know about, and it's my secrets he wants to share in.

"Okay, let me think." I look up the street, and the towering thick solid stone walls of Edinburgh Castle are just visible. I begin slowly. "When I was little, I wanted to be a princess when I grew up. Living in a castle like Edinburgh with a handsome prince. I had every Disney princess costume hanging in my walk-in closet. On weekends, I would choose a princess dress, and for that day, I would be that princess."

He laughs. "Please tell me you made your brothers dress up with you. I could just see you insisting they wear princess dresses."

"No way. They were all too big and would have ripped my dresses." I pretend to shudder dramatically, and he laughs harder.

"The most shocking thing about your story is that as a kid, you had a walk-in closet."

"Would it be shocking if I told you I still have all my princess dresses packed away in storage?"

"Aye, that is shocking. And I'm sorry to disappoint you, but there's no royalty in my family history, so no Scottish castles. The Stewarts were the monarchs who once owned Edinburgh Castle. The Campbells were more into pillaging and feuding with other clans. It made us very unpopular. There are even some parts of Scotland today where, as a Campbell, I'm not welcome."

"Really? I had no idea. But that's not a properly shocking personal story."

He grins, and it's so sexy I'm swooning like the ladies waiting at his book signings. Maybe we should turn around and walk back to the hotel so I can get him naked again.

"All right, prepare to be shocked. You know my friend Aaron and I joined the Royal Marines together when we were eighteen. Anyway, there was one night shortly after arriving back from a deployment in Iraq that we stupidly decided on a night off to wear our kilts out on the town. We got steamin' drunk and ended up flashing the entire crowded pub our bare arses and everything else."

I stop walking and turn to face him. "What? How? I need more details."

Laughter dances in his eyes. "One of our friends bet that we wouldn't stand on the table and do the highland fling. It was an easy bet, and the pay in the Royal Marines wasn't that great."

"But how did you flash everything? Did you drop your boxers?"

He bursts out laughing, and it's a few minutes before he can speak again. "Baby, a true Scotsman doesn't wear anything under his kilt."

My mouth drops open when a visual of Drew wearing only a kilt pops into my head. That is something I'd love to see. "Umm. Do you still have a kilt?"

"Aye. I have a couple."

Reaching up, I drag his lips down to mine and kiss him hard. Right there on the sidewalk, with tourists walking around us and Edinburgh Castle in the background. Who needs a prince when I have my own hot Scot?

I run my hand over the short, spiky hair on the back of his head. It reminds me of last night when I held his head between my thighs.

"Can we go back to the hotel room now?"

"Aye, my love. That we can."

The glint in Drew's eye tells me he knows exactly what I'm thinking.

TWENTY-SIX

Drew

Back in London at the end of the book tour, Katie slips her key in the shiny brass lock of her front door and turns it. Pushing the heavy black gloss door inward, she steps over the threshold. I follow behind, carrying our bags.

She throws her keys into a bowl on a hall table, then turns, smiling. "Welcome to my home."

I look down the long, polished wood hallway to the staircase going up and the staircase going down. I walk a few steps farther inside and poke my head around the open doorway on my right. The room screams luxury. Heavy brocade cream drapes tied back with gold tasseled cords partially cover large double sash windows. It wouldn't look out of place on the cover of a glossy designer home magazine. But the more I look, the more I realize this is a warm, cozy room rather than a staged picture. The book on the smoky glass coffee table is well thumbed, and there's a half-burned candle beside it. Two large cream sofas that even I could lie on full length are arranged facing a white marble fireplace, and scattered on each sofa is an abundance of cushions in a variety of colors and fabrics, still holding imprints from having been leaned on. The cream carpet throughout looks thick and soft. I swear if you dropped something small on it, you'd never be able to find it again.

I turn back to her. "Shit, Katie, this place is huge. I mean, I knew your family was wealthy, but I thought you were more my kind of rich. Not this. Sorry, that's rude."

Her nose wrinkles cutely, and her hand comes out to rest on her hip. "Do you have a problem with me having more money than you?"

I reach my hands to her hips and pull her flush against my body. "No. I don't give a shit if you have no money or a truckload of the stuff. It's just that I never really thought about it much until I saw all this. All that matters is that I have you."

"Good, because that's exactly the way I see it too." The dark depths of her eyes pull me under.

"Your home is very nice. Are you going to give me a tour?"

Her fingers drag up the back of my head, through the short hair there, and my cock thickens. I love the feel of her nails clawing at my body. "Let's start with the bedroom," she announces with a cheeky grin teasing the corners of her glossy lips.

I'm not surprised by her suggestion. I love that my woman craves sex as much as I do. When she gets that glint in her eye and she starts dragging her nails on me, I know that's exactly what she has on her mind.

She takes my hand and leads me up the steep stairs. "My

bedroom is on the first floor, and on the second are the guest rooms. Downstairs is the kitchen and my study. The ground level, as you saw, was the living room and the formal dining." She finishes speaking as we arrive at the doorway of her bedroom.

A king-size bed draped in a rich gold fabric dominates the room; it's opulent with a modern twist. To the side of the bed is a small original fireplace, keeping with the ornate cornicing and ceiling rose that are typical of these Victorian townhouses. I like that the room retains some original features. In the corner is a plush armchair with a few items of clothing tossed on it. Again, it looks lived in, rather than like a show home. Katie kicks off her heels and struts across the cream carpet through a doorway. From here, it looks like a walk-in closet with an adjoining bathroom. It's luxury on a scale I'm not used to.

"Make yourself comfortable. I am," she calls out from somewhere in her closet. Being in Katie's world might take some getting used to, but as I told her before, all that matters is that I have her.

I wander in the direction of her muffled voice, wondering what her version of comfortable looks like.

***

Later that night, we're lying in her bed. We've just made love, and she is snuggled into my side.

I ask, "Do I get to meet my substitute?"

She looks up at me quizzically. "What do you mean? There's no substitute for you." The way her painted nail taps me on my bare chest has my cock twitching with interest.

"The vibrator you used when you were missing the real thing. I want to size up the competition." I waggle my eyebrows at her, and she giggles.

"I never realized you were so insecure. It's in the top drawer behind you," she says, pointing.

I stretch back to reach for the set of drawers behind me. "The top drawer, not the bottom one?" I question, my hand soon grabbing hold of the toy.

"Well, things were getting a little frustrating just before the book tour. It needed to be handy."

I groan. "I think after tonight, it can go back to the bottom drawer."

She smiles, and I rip the covers back, leaving her naked before me. "Hey! Why'd you do that?" she squeals.

"Because I want to see how this works. Now be a good girl and open for me."

She spreads her legs wide, her eyes darkening to velvety brown like a decadent seventy-percent chocolate you find only in specialty stores. My eyes run over the mounds of her breasts, down to the valley of her stomach, and farther to the junction of her creamy, smooth thighs.

How did I get to be such a lucky bastard to be able to call her mine?

I switch the vibrator on, clicking up through the settings to the highest. Her pretty pussy is already glistening in the low light of the bedside lamps. Briefly, I touch the hot pink buzzing toy directly on her clit, and her hips jolt up off the bed.

"You seem to like that. Maybe I should be jealous of your toy. Or maybe your toy could become our toy." The truth is, her reaction is turning me on, and I lift up from the bed so I can see her completely. I touch her again in the same spot but for a few seconds more, and a moan falls from her lips.

Katie continues to track my movements, and each time I touch her, she either nibbles on her bottom lip, clenches her fists, or grinds her hips into the bed on a soft moan. It's fucking hot being able to see every reaction, small or big, and hear every delicate sound she utters as she reaches for her release.

"Drew …" she begs when I take her to the crest again and pull the pink tip away just before she falls over the edge.

"Not yet, baby. Soon." I lean down, circling my tongue around one pebbled nipple, then suck it into my mouth before doing the same with the other one. Her breathing is coming in erratic pants as she tries to hold off her orgasm for me.

When I bring the tip of the toy to her clit again, she pleads, "I can't … Drew … please." I run it up the inside of her folds once, then twice, then firmly press it to her nub. It vibrates against her, drawing from her an explosion of sound as her body tenses with her orgasm. Her eyes flutter closed, and I've never seen anything more beautiful than the look of ecstasy on her face.

How have I missed this before? When I've had my face buried between her thighs or I'm so caught up in my own pleasure, I feel like I've only seen moments. Now I can see her fully lose control. With my other hand, I wrap my fist around my cock and pump it hard. I'm so fucking turned on by the glorious woman beneath me.

I can't hold back. I can't stop it. I'm coming in thick streams across her tits, losing control just like she did.

When I can focus again, I look down, and Katie is grinning broadly, her eyes sparkling with pleasure. "It looks like my magic wand works for both of us."

"It seems that way. I vote we keep your magic wand in the top drawer." She drops her head back onto the pillow, laughing.

"Come on, my love. Let's get you cleaned up in that impressive high-tech shower I saw in your bathroom." I stand up, grab my T-shirt from the floor, and wipe my cum from her body. Then, holding out my hand, I lift her to standing. When she's on her feet, I tug on her hand and she falls against me.

She throws her arms around my neck. "Will you wash my hair for me?" she asks.

"Aye, it would be my pleasure."

Holding her tightly to me, I look down into her upturned face. "I love you, Katie." I dip my head to touch hers. "I want every breath to hold your sweet, fruity scent, every new adventure to have you by my side, and every night, I want to immerse myself in your beauty."

Her sharp intake of breath is barely audible, but I feel it.

She leans back. Her eyes are deep, reflective pools of unshed tears when she brings her hands up to my face. "I love you too, Drew."

My heart stutters.

Once …

Twice …

Then pounds back to life. How did I ever consider something less than everything with this woman? When everything about Katie is perfect.

EPILOGUE

Katie

Four Months Later

"Hip, hip, hooray. Hip, hip, hooray. Hip, hip, hooray."

Drew leans in to kiss my cheek, and smiling, I cut the two-tiered, dark-chocolate-covered cake, trying to avoid the cute little sugar daisies tumbling down the side of it.

Another cheer goes up, and my brothers' voices rise above the rest of the crowd.

I look around at the faces of those closest to me. My mom and dad, and next to them, Hunter, with his arm slung across the shoulders of Trudy. Since they became a couple at the beginning of the year, Hunter has not stopped smiling. Beside Trudy is Bec, tucked under the arm of Blake, her left hand resting on Blake's sleeve, the enormous solitaire diamond on her ring finger sparkling as brightly as the chandeliers hanging above us. Then there's Logan, laughing at something Blake just said to him. A few steps away are my girls, Allie, Sarah, and Dana, looking like a set of precious sparkling jewels in their pretty cocktail dresses, all three of them holding up their glasses of champagne in a toast to me.

I'm a little overwhelmed by the love of my family and friends in the room. And this was all possible because of the wonderful man beside me who organized my surprise party. I turn to Drew, and taking his face between my hands, I pull his lips down to mine. It's a steamy, hot kiss, full of promises of more, like all of Drew's kisses are. I could get lost in one of his kisses.

An ear-piercing whistle from Blake reminds us of where we are.

Reluctantly, I release Drew's lips. "This is the most amazing surprise birthday party ever. I have no idea how you managed to pull this off without me suspecting anything."

He laughs. "You forget I was trained to do covert operations. Besides I had a lot of help from your friends and your brothers. They're a sneaky bunch."

I look over at the girls, who are now talking to Drew's friend Aaron. "Well, I'm glad of their sneakiness. It was the best surprise. Thank you, and if I haven't mentioned it already at least fifty times today, I love you."

He drops another light kiss on my lips, then leans his forehead against mine. "I love you too, baby." His hands rest possessively on my hips, and the heat of his touch is already making me want to grab him by the hand and find somewhere private.

Originally, I thought tonight's plan was for us to have dinner in the hotel dining room with Allie, Sarah, and Dana, who had come to London to spend my birthday weekend with me. The big family celebration was going to be in a couple of weeks when Drew and I are booked to fly to New York. How wrong was I? This surprise party is so much more. Now my birthday weekend can be spent with my whole family and my best friends.

My head tilts to the side when I go to look up again at Drew. "I probably should have been suspicious when you insisted on making all the arrangements for dinner tonight. I did think you were planning something, like a cake." I look down at the delicious cake I just cut into. "I guess you did plan a cake. My favorite too, chocolate mud cake. Yum."

Picking up the knife from the table he cuts a bite-size piece and feeds it to me. "I aim to please," he growls. Eating cake from his fingers really shouldn't feel so erotic, but it does.

"Mmm. That tastes so good." I run my tongue over my lips to gather up the fudgy icing.

Drew's eyes lock onto my mouth, and he whispers in a low rough voice, "We might have to take a couple of slices up to our room for later because watching you eat from my fingers is fucking sexy."

I grin broadly, loving the power I have over this man. He might be full of surprises for my birthday but I have some of my own, for later. The new pale-pink lace underwear he hasn't seen yet will certainly play a major role in our private birthday celebration. Happy birthday to me.

"And will I have to wait till then to finally find out what a true Scotsman wears under his kilt?" I ask not for the first time tonight. I've been dying to know ever since Drew stepped out of our hotel room en suite dressed in the full formal regalia. I swear I nearly fainted at the sight of him. All I wanted to do was slip my hand under the traditional dark green and blue fabric to see exactly what Drew has on or more likely off under it. Instead, he rushed me out the door, saying we were late, and I didn't even get a chance to sneak a peek.

He laughs, throwing his head back.

Words cannot describe how sexy my hot Scotsman looks. It has to be said that his friend, Aaron, and brother, Rory, who are similarly dressed, look pretty fine too. They have certainly caught the attention of the single ladies in the room. Not surprisingly, Sarah was leading the charge. She grabbed me by the arm when she caught sight of them and quizzed me on their relationship statuses. Watch out boys, is all I've got to say on the matter.

***

Later that night, Drew and I are back in our room. The door bangs shut and I don't waste any time in dragging Drew's head down for a passionate, heart-racing, breath-stealing kiss. I pour all of my love for this amazing, wonderful man into this moment. This is how I wanted to kiss him when I walked into the function room filled with more than fifty of my friends and family all shouting "Happy birthday."

Eventually, I release his lips to say, "Thank you again, that was the best surprise ever." I run my hands down from his waist, over his tight butt cheeks on a voyage of discovery.

He chuckles, grabbing my wrists. "All in good time. But first I have one more surprise for you," Drew murmurs in his low sexy bedroom voice that never fails to send a shiver down my spine.

"I'm about all surprised out," I quip. It's been a huge day and night. I can't imagine what else he has in store for me. Actually, I can imagine and it involves the enormous bed behind me.

I tilt my head to the side and smile up at him. "Although I guess I could squeeze in one more surprise."

"You're going to like this one," he teases.

I move out of his arms and drop to sit on the end of the bed. "Come on then, Mister Campbell. Surprise away."

With a spin that flicks his kilt up a tantalizing smidge, he walks to his luggage and dives his hand into a side pocket. He retrieves a long white envelope and a small rectangular black box with a red ribbon tied around it. I don't remember seeing him put that there. I'm coming to realize that my boyfriend is as good at keeping secrets as my friends and family. He returns to stand in front of me, then hands me the envelope.

"This is all very mysterious," I say, looking up at him.

He's grinning from ear to ear. "Open it." His gray-blue eyes are wrinkled in merriment.

I carefully open the envelope and inside is a single sheet of white paper. Taking it out, I unfold it, then begin to read. It's a copy of a deed to a property in Cornwall.

My head springs up. "What? Is this the cottage?" He nods and his grin is even wider.

I gasp. "This says I own the cottage in Cornwall." He nods again. I drop the paper, jump up, throw my arms around his neck, and kiss him all over his face.

In between the sloppy wet kisses, I stutter out, "I can't believe … you bought me the cottage … in Cornwall. I love that place ... More importantly I love you."

"Aye, I know and I love you too. Now sit back down because there is one more part to the present." I sit down and he places the black box in my hand. "Happy birthday," he says again.

The box is the same size as the one Hunter and Trudy gave me earlier. That gift contained a gorgeous set of diamond earrings. However, this box is a lot heavier than I'd expect for jewelry. I arch my brows and gently shake the box close to my ear. It doesn't rattle but something shifts about inside.

He laughs at my attempts to guess what's in the box. "Go on, open it," he encourages.

I pull on the end of the red satin ribbon and it drops away. I lift the lid and inside is a smaller parcel wrapped in red tissue paper. Taking it out I carefully begin to pull away the paper. I can't even tell if the item is delicate or not. The final fold reveals a gold keyring with two keys on it. I lift it out and dangling from the keys on a thinner red ribbon is a ring.

I look up, my mouth wide open.

EPILOGUE

Drew

I take a knee before Katie, enclosing my hand around her one that is holding the keys and ring.

"Katie, my love, I know we said we'd wait but I don't want to wait another day. I want you to be mine completely and forever. I've known since Edinburgh we belong together. This last year I've learned that life can change quickly and you need to live every day like it's your last. I want every one of my days to be with you."

I stop to clear the lump in my throat before continuing, "Katie, I love you. Will you please marry me?"

Her mouth is still open and worryingly silent. "Katie, now is one of those times you need to use your words. You're killing me here."

She chokes out one word on a sob, "Yes." And it's all I need to hear.

I stand and draw her up to standing too. My arms wrap tightly around her shoulders, her arms looping around my waist while she buries her face into my shirt. I never expected proposing to my beautiful, strong, boss lady would reduce her to tears. Or me too for that matter. We stay like this for a few minutes, embracing until her tears dry and she lifts her head to look up at me.

She laughs gently. "I'm sorry for completely losing it. I want my every day with you too. I love you so much." Her voice cracks on those last words. "Sorry. I never expected this. I'm a little overwhelmed."

I smile down at her, then drop a light kiss to her lips. "I'm just glad you agreed. After speaking to your mum and dad yesterday I never expected asking you would be so nerve wracking."

"You spoke to my mom and dad?"

I nod. "I met them around the corner from our place yesterday morning, instead of going for a run like I said. We talked about the arrangements for tonight and I told them I'd be asking you to marry me after the party."

"Wow, you really are a traditional guy. I like that."

When I did the promised American book tour with Katie in the spring, we spent a couple of weekends with her family at their beach house in Southampton. Her mom and dad welcomed me warmly into the family from the moment I stepped through the door. Meeting her brothers again was a little more daunting but a few drinks and laughs together and we were fine. Although each of them did threaten my manhood if I did anything to hurt their little sister.

She looks up at me, her eyes deep dark liquid pools. "I'll send them a text to tell them I said yes. But first …" She reaches her hands low, her fingers slipping under the hem of the tartan fabric of my kilt, then ever so slowly creeps up the outside of my thighs.

I don't stop her this time. I'm looking forward to her discovering another way that I'm a traditionalist. Like a true Scotsman, there is nothing stopping her from wrapping those fingers around my hard cock.

It's a long while after that we are lying naked in the large bed, Katie's body tucked into my side, exactly where she belongs. Her left hand held out above us, with the large princess cut diamond sparkling in the lamp light while she waves it from left to right.

"This ring is so beautiful and fits perfectly." She places her hand back on my chest, over my heart.

I sigh contentedly. "Aye. It's your princess ring, and you can keep flashing it around. I want everyone to know your mine."

She slaps me playfully and I can't help smiling. It feels like a permanent state now that Katie is wearing my ring.

The last couple of months have been crazy, and the sense of relief washing over me is like being hit by a tidal wave. She said yes. My beautiful, clever, sexy woman agreed to be my wife.

From the first time Katie mentioned her birthday during the book tour in the States, it had me thinking. What do you get the woman who can buy anything? The answer, something priceless. And the one thing you can't buy is forever love. And I've got that in abundance for her.

Organizing the surprise party was big but nothing compared to the proposal. When the idea to buy the cottage came to me, I had my mission, and I didn't waste any time in setting the wheels in motion. I knew the landlord, Mary was looking to sell this year, and it was easy to make that happen once I let her know it was a gift for Katie. *One of her favorite people*, she told me. Finding the perfect ring was a lot harder and honestly, gave me more sleepless nights.

I think back to all those sliding doors moments that have bought me from the night on the dance floor when Katie fell into my arms, to this one, right now. I'm a lucky bastard.

Lucky to have spotted Katie on the dance floor that first night, when I'd been on my way out.

Lucky to have her fall into my arms and not some other guy.

But more than anything, lucky Katie accepted my love after I totally fucked up and pushed her away in Cornwall. Definitely one of my stupidest moments.

It's been a year since Cornwall, and I'm looking forward to returning with her, sometime soon. If it was possible, I'd whisk her off there tomorrow. But I know how excited Katie is to spend the weekend with our family and friends, even more now that she has the news of our engagement to share.

I tuck her closer into my body and begin to slowly stroke my palm over the smooth, soft skin of her arm, then down to her hip. She shivers in my arms. Tonight is just about us and there's hours still till we need to be meeting everyone for breakfast.

Hours for me to be making love to my bonnie lass, my fiancée.

The End

ACKNOWLEDGEMENTS

Eluding the Billionaire was a labor of love. I loved writing a story based around my favorite places in the United Kingdom. I loved the idea of a remote cottage overlooking the ocean to escape to. And finally, I loved creating a hero with a sexy Scottish accent.

I lived in the UK for about twelve years and came home to Australia with my very own Brit. Not a Scot but an Englishman who stole my heart and all these years later, still has it. I couldn't do any of this without the support and encouragement of my husband and three children.

As usual I offer my effusive thanks for you, my readers. Without you I would still only be writing technical system documentation. Yes that's my day job. Writing steamy contemporary romance is a lot more fun.

Thank you as always to my wonderful niece author JA Low, who has encouraged and guided me through this amazing journey.

Thank you to my friends who support me with coffee catchups or cocktails. Who listen to my story ideas and make suggestions of names and places.

Thank you to the many new author friends I have made over the last year. Most of whom I have never met in person but are a constant encouraging force for good. The author community really is a special group of lovely people.

Finally, a huge thank you to my team. My beta readers Joscelyn and Courtney, who keep my characters fresh, likable and interesting when I get bogged down in the detail, use the wrong words or take the story off down a rabbit hole. My editor, Beth and proofreader, Nicole who know everything I don't and probably never will, about grammar and punctuation. My talented cover designer Sarah, who remains tolerant of my many changes and at times total indecision. I appreciate the time, effort and care you have all put in to help me to bring my story to life.

Thank you.
Cate XO

ABOUT CATE

Cate Lane writes contemporary romance about swoony billionaire businessmen in custom-made suits, and hot military heroes, who find their HEA with strong independent women. All of her novels bring the heat and are standalone stories within an interconnected series.

She lives out her own happy ever after in Sydney, Australia with her husband and three children. When she's not writing, she likes to spend her time on beautiful beaches reading books or dreaming up new stories.

Sign up for Cate's newsletter to stay up to date on the latest news about new releases and bonus epilogues. Newsletter subscribers will be the first to receive bonus content, the latest news, teasers and release information. www.catelanebooks.com/newsletter

ALSO BY CATE

The CARLSON DYNASTY series

Satisfying the Billionaire (Book One)

What happens when the satisfaction of a no-strings-attached lover ends up tying me in knots?

Maybe it's time for some rope play.

Eluding the Billionaire (Book Two)

Dealing with one arrogant author making demands on my time is all part of the job. But when the author turns out to be my hot one-night stand, a publishing contract is the last thing I'm thinking.

And all I want to know is, *why did he leave that night*?

Seducing the Billionaire (Book Three)

What was I thinking?

Under duress, I agreed to let my sister's best friend stay in my spare room.

Only four weeks, she'd said. And that was twenty-eight days too long.

Gifting the Billionaire (A Christmas Novella)

Just friends … Well, that's what I thought we were,

until the night of the Carlson Christmas Charity Gala.

***

The LOVERS IN THE CITY series

Broken Lovers (Book One)

If heartache had a name, it would be Luke Steele ...

Forbidden Lovers (Book Two)

Some rules are meant to be broken.

Onetime Lovers (Book Three)

Maybe once will never be enough.

When One-time is so good they keep coming back for more.

Snowbound Lovers (A Christmas Novella)

Fireworks go off in the cold mountain air

of Aspen and it's not even New Year's Eve.

CATE LANE

BILLIONAIRE ALPHAS CONTEMPORARY ROMANCE

Made in the USA
Columbia, SC
13 April 2025

56563717R00126